The Last
Thursday Ritual
in
Little Piddlington

Maggie Shaw

The Last
Thursday Ritual
in
Little Piddlington

Maggie Shaw

eregendal.com

Also by the Author

The Vision and Beyond
(After the Night of Fires)

Diviner's Nemesis I – Avenger

Diviner's Nemesis II – Retribution

The Eagle and The Butterfly

First published in the United Kingdom in 2021
eregendal.com, Crewe, Cheshire
Printed in the United Kingdom by Lulu.com

ISBN 978-1-8381313-3-3 (paperback)

Contents

Illustrations

The Village Shop

INTRODUCTION and ACKNOWLEDGEMENTS

The Last Thursday Ritual in Little Piddlington is a humorous tale with a tongue-in-cheek moral, set in a remote English village in 1983. Miss Susy, the local good-time girl, longs for a wedding ring. Heir to Lodge Castle, Freddie says only when the Thursday Ritual ends. Can Susy stop the heist to become the new Lady of the Manor?

What is this ritual? Every fortnight, the Royal Mail delivers a large sum of money to the Little Piddlington Post Office to pay villagers their benefits and pensions. Also every fortnight, several teams of locals compete to steal the money before the payments can be made. Usually none of the teams are successful: will Thursday 15th September 1983 be different?

This madcap tale has a large cast of oddball characters and a style reminiscent of past comedy stalwarts like *The Goons*, *Monty Python's Flying Circus* and *Beyond the Fringe.*

The original story was written in the 1980s as a radio play for eight versatile actors. Some of its characters express prejudices often heard at that time, which thankfully are no longer considered acceptable. As in a radio play, the narrative moves swiftly from scene to scene to build into a compelling story.

Author Maggie Shaw has converted the original drama to this novel in a marked change of style for Eregendal, to entertain a new generation with its acerbic wit.

Many thanks go to Helen Lamb and Roy Butler for their assistance with the manuscript. Any faults in the work are the author's alone.

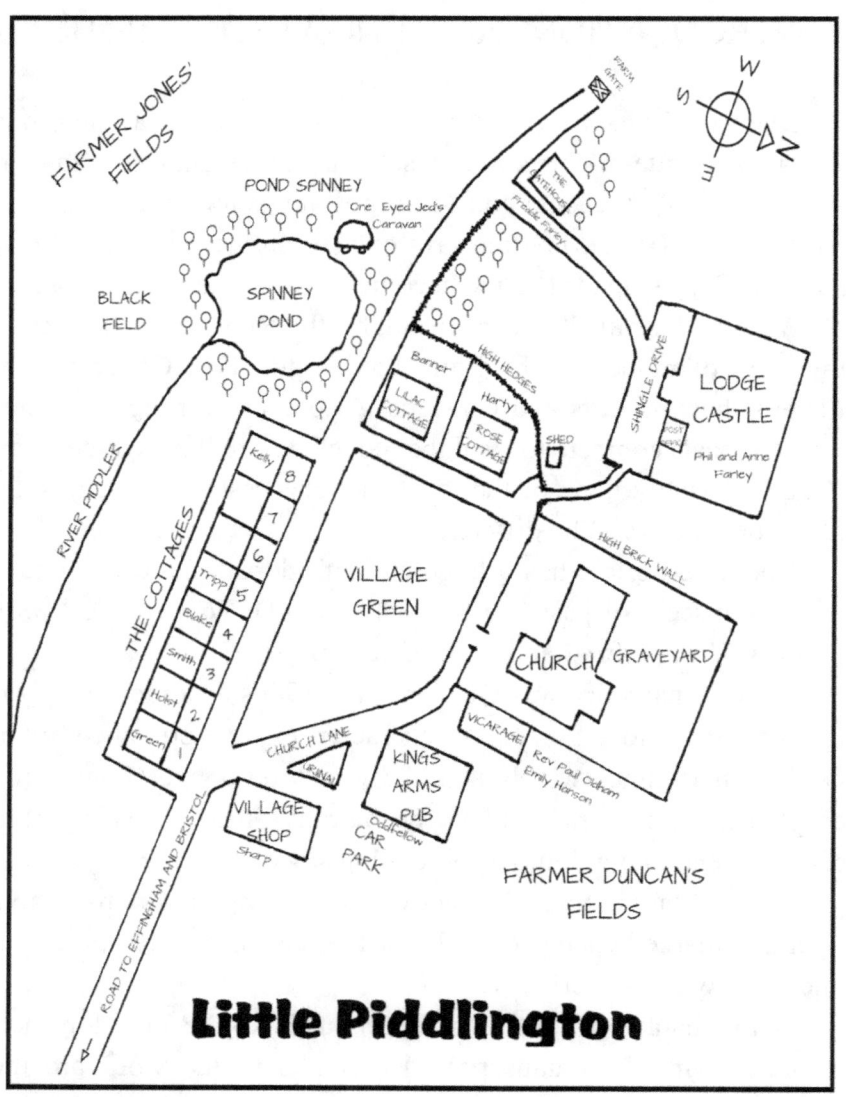

Little Piddlington

The Teams

The Reprobates
Matt Holst
One Eyed Jed

The Church
Revd Paul Oldham (Vicar)
Miss Emily Hanson

The Pub Regulars
Mike Smith
Smiley Winters
PC Tanner
Kev Kelly
Keith Kelly
+ Little Joey K

The Undertakers
Sam McNab
Pete Green
The Pallbearers
Jack Smith
Dave Tripp

The Down Effingham Brass Band with Pat Sewell

The Parish Council
Ted Banner
Major Harty
Simon "Sharkie" Sharp
Mr Gary Blake
Farmer Duncan

The Women's Institute
Mrs Gwendoline Harty
Mrs Rosie Banner
Mrs Sarah Sharp
Mrs Jennifer Blake
Mrs Maud Duncan
Mrs Mabel McNab
Mrs Jane Smith

The Up Effingham Morris Men

The Opposition

Lodge Castle P.O.
Freddie Farley
Miss Susy Sharp
Phil Farley
Mrs Anne Farley

The General Post Office
Bates
Belling

MAGGIE SHAW

The Cottages

Chapter 1: Welcome to Little Piddlington

1 : 1

It was a typical autumnal evening in the remote village of Little Piddlington. Not one sign hinted that the seeds of irreversible change were being sown.

This agricultural community had grown up at the end of a winding country road to nowhere, somewhere in the hills to the east of Bristol. Its sturdy honey stone and slate buildings gathered around a much-loved village green.

Mrs Holst was out as usual, standing stoically in the doorway of number 2, The Cottages, her plump arms crossed, waiting for her worse half Matt to come home. She had stood there for two years, waiting with a rolling pin in one hand, a resolute expression on her grim face, her floral overall washed to a colour almost as grey as her greasy hair. Meanwhile, her husband Matt had rented a room in the King's Arms inn across the road and lay on his bed taking potshots at her with an air rifle which he never got around to loading.

Across the village green, the church clock chimed five. The sultry evening air shimmered with familiar, poignant country sounds: the colourful calls of the herdsman bringing in his cattle to be milked, the sporadic splash of water flushing the automatic urinal, the buzzing reception of a badly tuned radio, the plaintive one-note melody of a penny whistle deliberately sat upon by a distraught mother, the occasional footfall of a weary worker or ten stampeding to the pub after a hard day's search for work; and down in Pond Spinney, One Eyed Jed's missus smashing the washing up on the caravan floor while Jed watched Miss Susy and her latest in the rushes. That see-through eye patch had been a godsend.

Little Joey K slipped his penny whistle into his back pocket and took aim with his catapult. He was an obnoxious ten-year-old with enough tricks up his ragged sleeves to send even the Vicar round the bend. That evening he did, too. Ash blonde Miss Susy sat up indignantly as her escort was flushed from cover.

'Ooh! All that trouble, and not even a blessing!' she sighed, straightening her denim mini-skirt. She was cultivating a relationship with the Vicar, and with every other available man in the village, because she longed for respectability, and thought she could only gain it with a wedding ring and the title "Mrs".

Reverend Paul Oldham shot off towards the road. As he passed Jed's caravan, he did not even stop to say his usual, 'Nice evening for a jog.' He ran so fast he could have set a new county sprint record.

One Eyed Jed chuckled to himself and knocked his cherry-wood pipe out into his wife's tea, which often happened when he wore his patch over the wrong eye. He was a tall, lean, stooped pensioner and wore a grubby mac whatever the weather.

'Get out, I say!' screamed his buxom wife. She looked not unlike Mrs Holst and was indeed her sister. As usual, she wore a well-washed floral cotton housecoat and slippers and kept her grey hair in curlers under a flowery pink headscarf. To emphasise her point, she smashed their last dinner plate on the corner of the table.

'Happy to oblige, dear,' Jed said, still chuckling. He stood up and put on the first hat his fingers touched, a deep purple bonnet with plastic flowers stitched into the hatband.

'And where do you think you're going in my best Sunday bonnet?'

One Eyed Jed opened the caravan door and shuffled down the steps.

'Over to the Queen's Legs, to see Matt Holst.'

A pudding bowl followed him out.

Pond Spinney is one of those places whose true worth will only be appreciated in a thousand years' time, when archaeologists attempt to reconstruct living conditions in the twentieth century. Placed amongst the trees and shrubs, hidden in the rampant brambles, and scattered along the reedy water's edge, were all the paraphernalia of modern built-in obsolescence: the washing machines and refrigerators, the microwave ovens and tumble driers, the cookers and food mixers, the heaters, radios, televisions, prams, pushchairs and sunbeds which had all been indispensable acquisitions until they went wrong and would each cost the same again to repair. Scattered among them were bottles and crisp packets and non-biodegradable plastic bags full of hedge clippings; while in the dark mysterious oil-slicked waters of the pond itself, rusted away a car of almost every model since 1928, excluding a Rolls Royce or two and the Ferraris.

In amongst the beer can bushes and paper bag trees shuffled One Eyed Jed, making a beeline for Miss Susy as she finished straightening her skirt.

'Harr, evening, Miss Susy.'

She spun round, startled, but relaxed to see the harmless old voyeur.

'Oh, it's you, Jed. You gave me quite a turn,' she said and giggled.

She was an attractive young woman, if one made allowances for the unusual shade of hair and face-pack make-up, the bright pink clothes, the lack of meat on the bones, and the grating high-pitched squeak in the timbre of her voice. But considering the nature of the men in Little Piddlington, why should she try to be perfect?

'What are you looking at me with your patch like that for, Jed?' she flirted.

'I'm not. I be looking at young Joey K with my blind eye.'

'Then how can you see where you're going?'

One Eyed Jed just chuckled and shuffled off along the rubbish-strewn path towards the village green.

1 : 2

In the pub across the village green, the landlord of the King's Arms was hard at work alone in his saloon bar prior to the 5.30 pm opening time, practising for the evening session. The pub was one of those rambling country inn hostelries with small rooms radiating in all directions around a central bar. Publican Tom Oddfellow was a thickset man in his forties, with stubble hair and clothes which hinted that he had no wife. The white of his creased striped shirt was grey and his beige work trousers had not been inside a washing machine for several months.

'Same again,' Tom ordered in a gruff West Country take off of an American accent, trying not to move his lips.

'Coming right up,' he replied brightly, pouring the contents of an empty bottle into a chipped whisky tumbler which he shoved along the polished counter. It slithered off the end and smashed on the floor.

Three loud knocks sounded on the saloon bar door. Tom Oddfellow looked up, startled to have his routine interrupted.

'Go away, stranger: this town ain't big enough for the both of us! It's not five thirty yet, either. Same again. Coming right up.'

Chink, slither, crash.

The saloon door burst open as the tumbler dropped. In surged a thirsty crowd of pub customers, followed more slowly by One Eyed Jed. Their noisy chatter hushed as he advanced across the saloon. Tom cringed behind the bar in the face of potential confrontation.

'Evening, Tom,' said Jed: 'See you've been watching a John Wayne film again, then. Just thought I'd let your regulars in out the cold: might as well be waiting in here as out there.'

'Well, you can just put them out, you old stirrer. And take yourself with them. You won't get a drink out of me!'

'Wouldn't ask you for one, Tom. Only came to see Matt Holst.'

Jed touched his wife's best Sunday bonnet and shuffled out through the door beside the bar, on his way to the upper floor.

The door beside the bar carried the inscription *Privet* in red chalk, in memory of the original writer, Old Sam Sowerby, at his hundredth birthday celebration. He had got confused between the words 'private' and 'privy': so confused indeed that he was still shouting out 'privet' next day when McNab the Undertaker was nailing him down in his coffin. An ancient law had been reinstated by the Parish Council, making it illegal for any villager to be older than ninety-nine. The law had not yet deleted the venerable Chairman, old Ted Banner. He deducted a year on each birthday, and at the rate he was going, would have to start work again in three years' time.

One Eyed Jed climbed the dark creaking staircase and shuffled along the dark creaking landing, looking for Matt Holst. The dull click of an air rifle told him where to go. He threw aside the heavy panelled door, stepped back to avoid its rebound against the sink, and entered the dingy bedroom. The door handle fell to the floor, broken.

'That you, Jed?' Matt asked, not stirring from his bed.

Matt was ten years younger than Jed and had gone to seed since moving into the pub. With his regular pension, he had no need to work, and lay in vest and slacks on his unmade bed all day, drinking and taking potshots at his wife with the unloaded air rifle.

Jed threw the door shut: it was the only way he could get it to move at all. He picked up the broken door handle and handed it to Matt, who dropped it beside his legs on the bed.

'It is, Matt. You still trying to make that gun fire?'

'I am that, Jed. What news?'

Jed took off his wife's best Sunday bonnet and hung it on the hook behind the door. After he turned away, the hook dropped the hat on the floor.

'Your wife's still out there, Matt.'

'Don't I know it, Jed. Two years she's been standing there with that rolling pin in her fist, and won't even say what I've done wrong.'

'Harr, women be a bit funny about a man having a few. You just get shot of her and have done with it.'

'That's what I'm trying to do, Jed. See…?'

Matt raised the rifle, took aim and fired. The trigger clicked ineffectively.

'… These pellets are useless.'

'Well, I told you not to buy 'em from Sharkie Sharp's village shop. What about a drink, then?'

'Help yourself, Jed. Tap marked W. I'll have one too.'

Jed picked up a couple of tooth mugs from the floor. He rinsed them out at one sink tap and filled them from the other.

'You thought any more about the Post Office?' he asked and handed Matt his drink.

Matt nodded and lay back with eyes closed to sip the pale liquid from the glass. The bland taste made him sit up again, spluttering.

'Hot water? I said the tap marked W for Whisky, you old fool, not H for Hooch. You got your patch on the wrong eye again?'

One Eyed Jed gave a suggestive chuckle.

'Harr: been bird spotting again. That new Vicar be a fast mover, harr!'

Matt got to his feet and snatched Jed's drink from his hand.

'Here, give me your glass. And put your patch on the right eye for once!'

He emptied the two glasses down the sink and filled them again with a clear amber liquid from the tap marked W. Jed picked up the weapon he had left on the bed.

'Harr, this be a gay fine-looking air rifle.'

'If only it worked! Hey, don't you point it at me, you old fool!'

Jed raised the muzzle upwards and fired. A pellet smashed the light bulb above their heads.

'So it do work. And it shoots straight,' Jed said.

'Fine! Now what do we do with no light bulb? No, don't answer! Have a glass of the marvel of Tom Oddfellow's still instead.'

They both raised their tooth mugs and drank a deep draught of the amber brew. One Eyed Jed smacked his lips.

'Harr! That's a gay fine drop of whiskey he brews,' he said.

He raised the air rifle and pointed the muzzle at a target outside the window.

'Hey, what are you aiming at now?' Matt asked, alarmed.

'Just seeing if I'm a better shot than you, Matt.'

A sudden strange silence struck the village. The Water Board had cut off the village water supply, Mother Kelly had crushed Joey K's penny whistle, and One Eyed Jed's missus had smashed the last piece of crockery in the caravan. Little Piddlington had been struck dumb.

An air gun pellet smashed through the glass window, shattering the silence. Mrs Holst screamed and dropped to the ground outside the front door of number 2, The Cottages. As she fell, the church clock struck the quarter hour. Jed studied her lifeless body for a few moments. When she still did not move, he spoke on.

'Hmm. Looks like you can go back home now, Matt.'

Matt joined him at the broken window, his slippers crunching on the shards of glass. He looked down at his wife's body and toasted her fall with stolen whiskey.

'So we've finally got shot of her then.'

He paused and took another sip of whiskey. There was a lot to consider when facing the prospect of going back home. At length he shook his head.

'No, I'm better off staying here; if I can mend the window and the light, that is. I don't have enough copper pipe to supply my house from Oddfellow's still. Look out: here come the vultures.'

Across the green from the pub, the front doors of two more terraced cottages sprung open.

'Ooh! Mrs Holst!' exclaimed Mrs Jane Smith at number 3, The Cottages. She was a petite, birdlike woman with a practical nature, big hair to make her look daintier, and Dolly Parton-style everyday clothes.

'What's happened, Mrs Smith?' asked Mrs Pamela Green at number 1, The Cottages. A pinny covered her Marks & Spencer skirt and blouse, and her arms were covered in flour up to her elbows.

'I dunno, Mrs Green,' said Mrs Smith. 'I was just standing in the hall, looking through the letterbox, when there was this awful crash and Mrs Holst screamed. She doesn't look very well, does she?'

'She's not moving much, either. Must have tripped on the step.'

'Yes, you can see the blood where she hit her head on the path.'

'I wonder if she's dead, Mrs Smith.'

The front door of number 4, The Cottages sprang open and Mrs Jennifer Blake bounced out. She covered her well-endowed body with a mid-blue shirtdress and her muscular legs were bare but for sensible black brogues. Her shoulder-length blonde hair was pulled back from her homely face in a ponytail.

'Hello, ladies. Anything I can do?' she asked, radiating energy.

'Don't think so, Mrs Blake. It's just Mrs Holst, dropped dead on her doorstep,' said Mrs Smith. She sounded as if things like that happened there all the time.

'What a pity. Such a nice woman. Except for the colour of her curtains.' This remark arose from their not being in Mrs Blake's favourite blue, but in a bright orange fashionable in the 1970s.

'Should we phone someone?' asked Mrs Green.

'No need. The dustmen will come round tomorrow,' said Mrs Smith.

'Fine, then. Must go. WI meeting tonight,' said Mrs Blake, and sprung back into her house. The door to number 4 swung shut behind her.

'And I can't stand round here gossiping all day, either, Mrs Green. Got to get ready for closing time,' said Mrs Smith.

'What's your latest idea, Mrs Smith? I never have any good ideas. Except my ten-foot hole by the front door, and I fell into that myself.'

'That's cos you're a groove thinker, Mrs Green. You've got to jump out of the grooves for good ideas. I'm toying with a plan to rig a trip wire to a ton of TNT. If it works, it'll blow the whole of Little Piddlington to Bristol.'

'What a good idea. They we could go shopping more easily. Why don't I think of ideas like that?'

'Only cos your brain's not connected up, Mrs Green.'

With that parting shot, Mrs Smith went back inside number 3, The Cottages and closed the front door. As she walked along the tiled hall to her kitchen, she muttered under her breath.

'She'd even believe a *Protect and Survive* handbook.'

Then she saw her nineteen-year-old daughter at the bread bin.

'Oi, Michelle,' she shouted: 'What are you doing in the kitchen?'

Slim, petite Michelle tossed her long black hair with an impatient tut. She was wearing her favourite leather trousers and a white silk shirt, and liked to be known as Mike.

'Just getting me tea, Mam. What's going on at Mrs Holst's?'

'Nothing much: she just died on her garden path. Hey! How much bread have you eaten?'

'Only half a loaf.'

'Only half a loaf? Michelle, you know I told you to cut down on food. It's not good for you. Why, you're six stone already! You should be dieting like the rest of us, tightening your belt. How else can we stop inflation?'

'Oh, shut it, Mam! You've been listening to a party political again. All this inflation waffle's a load of bull, just another Tory trick to con more out of us.'

She pulled her leather jacket off the back of a kitchen chair and stood up to leave.

'And where do you think you're going now, young lady?' demanded her mother.

'Over The Queen's Legs. Gotta see Smiley Winters.'

'I dunno. The youth of today, always going out. Why don't you stay at home and watch the box like any other self-respecting citizen?'

'Cos it's not very interesting since they cut off the electric.'

Michelle 'Mike' Smith donned her black leather jacket and marched out of number 3, The Cottages. With her black leather jackboots on, she stood over six feet tall. The other villagers often wondered how she managed to pedal her push-bike wearing ten-inch platform heels. She put her hands in her jacket pockets and plodded across the green in the direction of the village pub.

1 : 3

In the saloon bar of the King's Arms, the regulars sat waiting with their tongues hanging out, impatient for the clock to strike half-past five and mark legal opening time. Tom Oddfellow was still practising his John Wayne impression, using glasses from a box of factory rejects that had fallen off the back of a lorry.

'Same again. Coming right up!' Chink, slither, smash.

But now each time he sent a tumbler off the end of the bar, gentle giant Smiley Winters swept up the broken glass and put it in the bin. Swish, crunch.

Smiley Winters had the body of a bald gorilla, covered in well patched cowboy shirt and denims, both hand-me-downs from villagers who had no further use for them. His shaven head made him look a brute of a man mountain, but he had a real soft spot for Mike Smith. He beamed at her as she crossed the saloon to the bar. She winked at him and leaned against the counter.

'Same again. Coming right up.'

Chink, slither, thud.

Tom Oddfellow looked up in surprise at the change in sound.

'Oh! Er, hello Mike. Caught the glass, I see, ha, ha, ha! Only you scared me.'

'Sure, Tom. Anyone taller than you scares you. Not open yet?' She slid the glass back.

'The church clock hasn't rung half five yet.'

'It's slow.'

Beads of sweat appeared on the publican's broad brow.

'Oh. Er, is it, PC Tanner?' he asked.

PC Tanner joined them at the counter. Although he was out of uniform and wearing a jogging top and bottoms, his looks and manner told people as clearly as a neon sign what he did for a living.

'No, Mr Oddfellow,' he replied, referring to the clock.

'Then, Mike, I'm afraid, er...' Tom began.

'Sure, chicken: you scare easy. How about a nice round of drinks on the house? After all, we're all friends of yours, aren't we. At least, we should be after spending ninety per cent of the village earnings in here.'

'I can't do that, Mike. Can I, PC Tanner?'

'But you can, Mr Oddfellow.'

Tom blanched. 'All twenty of you?'

'Yes, Mr Oddfellow,' the policeman affirmed.

'The usual?' Tom asked hopefully.

'Sure, Tom,' Mike said: 'Treble scotch all round.'

'But…'

'Unless you want PC Tanner to see your cellar.'

The publican caved in and placed twenty whiskey glasses on the counter.

'Glad you're being sensible, Tom,' Mike said. She called out, 'Drinks on the house, everyone.' Then she turned back to Tom. 'Oh and don't forget yourself.'

The pub crowd stampeded to the counter to fight over the drinks Tom poured them. Mike picked up the first two but was jostled by one of Joey K's big brothers, Kev. He was a rough-looking farm labourer who had been signed off sick for four years with a bad back.

'Hey, don't you push me, Kelly!' she shouted and kneed him below the belt. He folded double as she passed. Then she called out to the man mountain. 'Hey, Smiley, come on over here. Let's take the corner table, get out of this mob.'

Smiley was at her side in an instant, clearing the way for her. Occasional undertaker's assistant Pete Green made the mistake of crossing into their path. Smiley barged him aside so forcefully, he bounced against the wall. A trail of winded bodies fell in their wake as he escorted Mike across the Saloon to a quieter corner.

'Where do you want this table taken to, Mike?' Smiley asked. The look on his moon-shaped face showed he was totally smitten.

'No, Smiley: when I said "let's take the corner table", I meant, let's sit here,' she replied, like a patient teacher explaining a hard fact to a struggling pupil.

Smiley sat on the bench seat by the wall as all the pub chairs were too small to accommodate his ample backside. Mike sat opposite him in a carver chair. The melee at the bar had quietened down. The thirsty crowd had all just got their drinks when the nearby church clock struck the half hour.

'Bar's open,' Tom Oddfellow called out in relief.

'Cheers, Mike. Thanks for the drink,' said Smiley. He looked down at the whiskey as if he had been told never to drink alcohol.

'Don't be frightened of it, Smiley. It won't bite you,' she said.

'But I only drink coke. And I get hangovers on that!'

'Never mind: we can't all be perfect. At least you're big and strong.'

Smiley nodded proudly. 'Like PC Tanner says, as stout as three brick walls, and twice as thick. What brings you in here, Mike?'

'My legs, Smiley, to see you.'

'To see me? Well, I never, Mike. You've made my day. Now you've seen me, should I go?' He looked like a scolded puppy at the thought.

'No, Smiley. You can help me.' Mike opened a cigarette packet and offered him one. 'Here, take a fag.'

'Taking a fag doesn't usually help people. Mr Oddfellow gets very cross if I take any of his.'

'No, Smiley, this is for us to smoke while we talk.'

She pulled two cigarettes out of the packet. One, she handed to Smiley; the other she placed between her thin lips. She flicked her lighter open, lit her own, and paused.

'Other end, Smiley. The filters don't make a good smoke.'

He turned his cigarette and copied the way she had lit hers. As the flame ignited the tip, he breathed deeply, filling his lungs with smoke. He coughed uncontrollably.

'Why don't you clear your throat with your drink, Smiley?' Mike suggested.

He gulped the whiskey and slammed down the glass, choking and coughing even more. With tears in his eyes, he said,

'This is the life, eh, Mike – just like the grownups do.'

A few wheezy breaths later, he finally asked, 'How can I help you, Mike?'

'Tomorrow's Thursday.'

'Really?'

'Tomorrow the Post Office gets all the cash for the pensions, the family allowances, the dole money, the supplementary benefits and any other Post Office transaction which can't be dealt with any other day of the week in Little Piddlington, there being no Post Office open on any other day. Correct?'

'You're talking too grand for the likes of me, Mike.'

'Okay, Smiley; in plain terms, tomorrow morning, the Post Office will give Mr Farley at Lodge Castle a thousand quid to hand out to all us poor unemployed. Right?'

'I wouldn't know how much it is...'

'Okay, forget that. Tomorrow, Phil Farley will have a lot of money at home.'

'Will he? Why?'

'Because it's Thursday.'

'Why not today because it's Wednesday?'

'Forget it, Smiley,' Mike said, her patience wearing thin:

'D'you want to earn a fiver?'

'Yes, please.'

'Good. Then tomorrow, you and me are...'

She paused as PC Tanner joined them at the table.

'Oh, hello, PC Tanner,' she said, her voice unenthusiastic.

'Gonna do the Post Office again this week, Mike?' he asked with a knowing tone.

'Sure. What of it?' she said, her head cocked in a belligerent sneer.

'I told you last week, Mike, and the week before, and the week before that. It's no good. Since Phil Farley was robbed three weeks running last year, he's tightened up. PO money out of Lodge Castle? I'd sooner get POWs out of Colditz.'

'Not this time. This time it's different. I've got a plan.'

'It was different last week, Mike, and you had a plan the week before. Each week it's different, you've got a plan.'

'This one's infallible.'

'Last week it was fool proof, and look where you ended up! I told you that secret passage from the cemetery led to the well.'

'Okay, okay. So this week I'm trying a whole new approach.'

'Oh yes? Like what?' PC Tanner sneered.

'Okay, don't believe me. Just kick yourself when you read all about it in tomorrow's Evening Packet.'

'All right, Mike.' PC Tanner sat down at the table. 'Count me in.'

'Tom,' Mike called across the bar: 'Same again for us three.'

'Coming right up,' Tom replied.

The publican pressed a whiskey glass to an unlabelled bar tap. To his consternation, nothing came out. He tried again, but still nothing came out. Mike saw his expression and came over to the bar to hurry him.

'I said, the same again, Tom!'

'And I said, it's coming, Mike.'

He turned to the bottles of spirits hanging behind the bar and pressed the three glasses against a whiskey optic to dispense three singles.

'My, my, Tom; the real thing for once! Here's fifty. You can keep the change!'

She threw a fifty pence piece on the counter and took the three drinks back to her table.

' "Keep the change", she says!' Tom muttered.

Concerned about his profit margins, Tom waited for the first opportunity to hurry down to his cellar and check his still.

1 : 4

Tom Oddfellow had to wait for the six thirty lull in the King's Arms before he went down to his cellar to check his still. He could not afford to keep giving his customers real whiskey at his cut-rate prices, but if he stopped serving cheap spirits, there would be a riot in the village.

Tom switched on the light and locked the heavy cellar door behind him. The bare 60-watt bulb struggled to light the room below. He stepped carefully down the damp stone staircase.

The large copper whiskey still rested on the flagstones in a corner of the cellar, softly bubbling. Two storage coppers stood beside it, one on either side. Nothing looked out of place as he checked the installation. He took down a tin mug from a wall hook to take a sample of the new batch as it dripped from the still before it dropped into the right-hand copper. Though the spirit tasted raw on his tongue, it was coming along well and would be ready next day, much to his relief.

Tom slapped the other big copper. It rang emptily, like a bell.

'So why did you run dry? I can't smell a leak.'

He checked the pipes connecting the systems more closely and noticed a metal pipe running up the wall from the empty copper to the floor above. All his supply pipes were plastic.

'So that's where Matt Holst gets it from! Just wait till I get him!'

He set about disconnecting the pipe.

Two storeys above him, the W tap ran dry. Matt Holst looked at its spout in consternation.

'I think young Tom's just cut off my supply, Jed,' said Matt: 'Maybe I will move back home tonight, after all.'

'Has he, Matt? Then we'll have to make do with water. We've a mite bit of planning left yet with this light blown, and rare little time to do it in.'

'I was thinking, it's time we did the pension dodge again. That way, Farley can't refuse us entry.'

'That's good thinking, Matt. But what are our chances?'

'Easier than taking candy off a baby. We just have to arrive there the same time as the Post Office van. When does that usually get to the village?'

Jed heard a rustling noise outside the broken window and moved closer to listen. The noise came from the ivy around the drainpipe by the window. He picked up the air rifle again.

'Eight thirty in the morning, Matt, though it's rarely on the dot,' he said, and fired.

'Aargh!' cried Joey K.

The boy fell from the drainpipe and landed with a thud in the flowerbed below. He lay on his back with his limbs spread out like a starfish. His face wore a brief mask of horror and shock.

Matt sprinted across the room, his feet crunching on the broken glass. He threw open the sash-cord window and leaned out to shake his fist at the boy.

'You little blighter, Joey K! You've been up that drainpipe again, listening in,' he swore.

'Harr, but he won't be listening in anymore,' said Jed. He checked the air rifle was empty and put it down on the floor.

Joey K scrambled to his feet below them. He raised his right forefingers in a traditional salute of contempt as he pulled out his catapult with his left hand.

'Don't you bet on it. He's just picked himself up and...'

Joey's missile hit its mark.

'Ouch! You bleeding blighter! That's my chin. Next time I hope you break your neck!' Matt shouted back.

Little Joey K ran off across the village green, pocketing his catapult. He ran home to number 8, The Cottages. In the back kitchen, his mother Mrs Kelly was laying the formica-topped table ready for his tea. She was a short buxom woman, clad in a drab pinafore over her cheap second-hand olive skirt and green cotton top. She had scraped her hair into an untidy bun at the nape of her neck.

'Home, Mam,' Joey called.

He slammed the front door and ran down the tiled passage into the kitchen.

'So I notice. What have you been up to, to get black as the ace of spades?' she demanded.

'Fell off a drainpipe. One Eyed Jed fired at me with Matt Holst's air rifle.'

Mrs Kelly banged some cheap Woolworths mugs and plates down on the table and splodged some bubbling baked beans onto two plates.

'You'll've deserved it, likely as not. Here's your tea.'

'Not beans again, Mam.'

'Beans are good for you.'

'But Mam, I 'ate beans.'

'If you don't want 'em, you can go without. Did you find out anything?'

Joey wolfed down three mouthfuls of beans. Then he answered, 'They're all at it again, just like last week.'

'Well, this week they'll have a little bit of competition from your two big brothers. It'll come in nice and handy for your father's coming out party. And how many times have I told you not to put your catapult in your back pocket? Stuff it up your jumper where they can't see it!'

'Aw, Mam! It's quicker on the draw there. And no-one does see it, not when it counts. Like I got Miss Susy's latest catch today, down by the pond.'

'Don't you talk like that about your cousin Susan! Who did she pull this time?'

'Only the Vicar!'

'Not the new Vicar, Paul Oldham?'

'Yup. Didn't know he could run that fast!'

Joey wolfed down some more beans and continued to tell the tale.

1 : 5

On the other side of the village green, in the chintzy surroundings of the Vicarage lounge, the Vicar described the same tale to his housekeeper with significant differences. Miss Emily Hanson was serving high tea from the tea trolley, her ample dimensions looking vast in the knitted beige fabric twinset she always wore.

'I certainly didn't know I could run that fast, Miss Hanson,' laughed the Vicar, a little embarrassed. He was a lean, earnest young man with a boyish, bespectacled face and a look of innocence. His single status attracted a lot of interest from the spinsters of the parish.

'What a shock for you, Vicar, and in the public convenience of all places!' she said. 'More tea, Vicar?'

'I wish you would stop saying that, Miss Hanson. But perhaps another fairy cake.'

'Wouldn't you rather have a rock cake?'

She offered the plate with a smirk.

'No, thank you. My jaw is still recovering from Mrs Farley's rock cakes. Which reminds me. I have been thinking of taking up Little Piddlington's most popular pastime myself.'

'Not getting tipsy in the Queen's Legs?' She looked appalled.

'Gosh, no, no, no, no, no! I meant, the Thursday Ritual. If only I could get such numbers coming to church each week.'

'If you managed to relieve the Post Office of its bankroll, they would come flocking.'

'But what about the eighth Commandment: *Thou shalt not*

steal?'

'We've paid our taxes all our working lives. We would only be taking what we've already paid in. And no-one would suffer. There's plenty more where that came from.'

The Vicar regarded Miss Hanson with a reproving look over his round wire spectacles.

'You've been thinking about this before, Miss Hanson, haven't you.'

'I must confess, I have, Vicar. I used to know Lodge Castle intimately.' Her smile became a look of scorn. 'And Mr Farley still owes me a very large favour. With his assistance, and providence on our side…'

'And a good plan?'

The Vicar's hopeful smile turned to one of regret.

'No, my motives are wrong. I can manage quite well on my push-bike, really.'

'Then put the money into the Church Roof Restoration Fund. That wouldn't be a selfish motive.'

'True. Since the Kelly boys stole the lead, I dread giving sermons when it's wet – that sea of umbrellas. And my surplices keep shrinking.'

For a few moments, a kaleidoscope of different expressions passed over his face. Then he came to a decision and nodded.

'All right, Miss Hanson. We'll do it. First, I need to know the layout of the land. What obstacles would we face?'

'Nothing that a little ingenuity cannot surmount.'

Miss Hanson pushed aside the tea trolley and pulled down the window blind to reveal a map of Lodge Castle. The housekeeper transformed herself into a teacher, complete with a bamboo pointer she had pulled out of a potted plant.

'Lodge Castle, as you know, is neither a lodge nor a castle,' she said: 'It is a fortified manor farm built in 1431 on the site of a pele tower by Philip Farley's ancestor, Lord Montague Smithson Farley. For a variety of reasons, the house has been demolished and rebuilt twelve times since then, and also extensively remodelled on twenty-three other occasions.'

'Sounds like they suffered from the Kelly boys too! But we are not at school now, Miss Hanson. Perhaps we could leave the history lesson.'

'Sorry, Vicar: I was getting carried away. I had always thought that one day Lodge Castle would be my home.'

'Yes. What a pity Mr Farley turned down all your Leap Year Day proposals, in favour of Mrs Farley. You are an excellent housekeeper. You would have made him a fine wife.'

Miss Hanson visibly preened herself at his praise.

'Do you really think so, Vicar? Thank you, thank you. Have some more tea.'

'No, er, not just yet, thank you. What about the obstacles, Miss Hanson?'

She raised the bamboo cane to point out relevant features on the window blind plan as she spoke further.

'Like the architecture of the building, its defences are also of many styles gathered together over the years. The tiled entrance hall has six trap doors concealed by white tiles. If an intruder steps on one of these, it folds downwards and deposits them in the cellar kitchen where Mrs Farley's frying pan awaits.'

'Formidable. No-one could withstand her attack.'

'Not so, Vicar. Mrs Farley is a pillar of the church. She would hardly strike you!'

'Even Boaz and Jachin were struck down, Miss Hanson. But perhaps if I wore my glasses…'

The telephone interrupted him. He set down his china cup and saucer and picked up the receiver. The call started with payphone pips. The caller had to insert some money before he could speak.

'Hi, there, Rev. Sam McNab the Undertaker here. We've got another customer,' he said, his deep voice slightly breathless.

'Another customer, Mr McNab?' the Vicar repeated, not used to such informality when talking about the dear departed.

'Yup: Matt Holst finally did it. The neighbours had left the body for the dustmen to collect tomorrow, but I nipped in smartish while Crossroads was on and picked up the stiff myself.'

'The stiff? Who was the poor unfortunate?'

'Holst's missus, of course. Her doc's already certified it as a heart attack. When can we do the last rites?'

'Well, I…'

'Thought tomorrow would be as good a time as any. Tomorrow morning, say, about eight thirty?'

'But I'll be busy then.'

'Fine. I'll see you tomorrow, then, eight thirty on the dot, at number 2, The Cottages. Goodbye.'

Sam McNab slammed down the phone and chuckled.

He stepped out of the public phone box near the church and crossed the road to the traffic island between the pub and the shop. Here, by public subscription, the Parish Council had erected an automatic flushing urinal to combat the problem of men committing nuisances each night after the Kings Arms had shut. Here too, some villagers had wanted a similar convenience to be erected for Man's best friends. Parish Council Chairman Ted Banner sidestepped this issue because a more extreme element had also demanded a similar facility for cattle, which would have turned the whole of the village centre into one vast latrine.

Pete Green already stood in the convenience, waiting for McNab. Pete's patience was somewhat strained as the water board had unexpectedly reconnected the water supply at twice the normal pressure. This had confused the valve on the automated tap. Instead of an occasional gentle flush down the porcelain when required, the water sprayed out without warning at a twenty-degree angle every couple of minutes.

'Get through, Sam?'

The water flushed again. Pete swore.

'Cor blimey! Need a bleeding raincoat in 'ere!'

'Never mind, Pete. By this time tomorrow it'll all have been worthwhile,' Sam said. 'I booked the funeral at eight thirty like we wanted. What with Lodge Castle's grounds being next to the graveyard...'

The water flushed again, obscuring some words.

'... with the full works, including the Down Effingham Brass Band. When the procession arrives at point X... What are you doing now, Pete?'

'Just taking advantage of the facilities, Sam.'

Sam studiously turned to look the other way.

'Sorry. As I was saying, when the procession arrives at point X, the band...' The water flushed again. '... Damn this flaming thing! New shoes, too – only had 'em a year. Five minutes before D time's when you come in, Pete. I've put you in charge of the pallbearers, so at that point, you'll get 'em to file the coffin in behind...'

The water flushed again.

Miss Susy swore and straightened up, taking her ear off the metal wall of the latrine. She was not normally the type to snoop on men's conveniences and had been trying to eavesdrop on their plans for a good cause. Her inability to hear what was being said annoyed her.

'Ooh! How can I listen in with all this racket going on!'

She marched off towards the church, her spindly heeled shoes clip-clopping on the pavement.

1 : 6

Miss Susy headed for The Gatehouse where her boyfriend Freddie Farley lived. They had had a casual relationship for several years, mainly through Susy's efforts. Though Freddie only lived in the Gatehouse now, she knew when his daddy died, he would get the rest of the estate too. If she played her cards right, one day all the Lodge Castle would be hers.

The Gatehouse was a two-roomed cottage standing among deciduous trees at the entrance to the Lodge Castle estate. Susy clip-clopped up the short flagstone path and knocked on the heavy dark oak door. When no-one answered, she turned the massive wrought iron door handle. The door creaked slowly open. Inside, the cottage was in darkness.

'Cooee! You there, Freddie?'

No-one answered. Susy ventured inside. The heavy door squealed shut behind her. Heavy maroon velvet curtains and dust deadened any sounds in the room. As Susy's eyes adjusted to the gloom, she looked at the messy living room in disgust.

'What a tip! He can't have cleaned this place in months. Freddie?'

She took four more steps and tripped over two legs she had not noticed in the shadows.

'Ooh! There you are, Freddie. What are you doing under the desk?'

'Couldn't find my bed,' he replied.

He emerged, sleepy-eyed, and turned on the desk lamp. The messy room became bathed in a golden glow.

Freddy was a thin, pale, weedy young man with unkept shoulder-length hair and mousy whiskers which looked like a failed attempt to grow a beard. He wore an unwashed, baggy, tie-dyed purple T-shirt and threadbare loon trousers, both fashion products from an earlier decade. Paint spatters stained his face and clothes.

'Catching up on your sleep again, Freddie?' Susy asked, and giggled.

She moved two paintings aside to clear a space on a chair.

'Hey, careful with those! What did you move them for?'

'I was only finding somewhere to sit. Have you been working on your masterpiece again?'

'Yes. How did you know?'

'Not everyone has an indigo nose.'

'Indigo? I only use Prussian blue.'

Susy sighed and flopped down on the chair she had cleared. Freddie leaned on the edge of the desk beside her.

'Indigo? Prussian? Blue? It's all the same to me, Freddie! It's you I like, not your paint pots. So what has my little master artist been up to today, hmm?'

Her fingers walked suggestively up his right forearm. He completely missed their meaning as she had asked him about his work. Energy and enthusiasm coursed through him as he remembered his latest creation.

'I've been painting a new pub sign. I had a great idea.'

He dug out a board from all the clutter and placed it on an easel. Then he turned on a spotlight so that she could admire his latest creation too.

'Tantara! What do you think?'

The painting depicted a furry garment decorated with false legs. Susy was astonished but not very impressed and did not know how to respond to his revelation.

'Oh, Freddie!' she said: 'What are all the legs for? And why are they all sticking out of what looks like my fur coat?'

'That was the stroke of genius! You know that pub sign on the way to Bristol, the King's Arms?'

'Where your lighter exploded in your pipe and your beard burnt off?'

'That's it. Remember the sign outside: the shield with all those funny patterns and a crown?'

'You mean, the coat of arms?'

'Yes! That's it, don't you see. King's Arms, coat of arms; Queen's legs, coat of legs!'

'Freddie, I don't wish to sound…'

'Don't worry. I can take being called a genius.'

'Oh, Freddie! "The Queen's Legs" is just a village joke. It's really called the King's Arms too.' She shook her head. 'Oh, why do I like you so much?'

'My boundless talent, my matchless good looks, my innate

modesty, and my father's millions.'

'Huh! I'll believe in all them when I see them!'

'Then what did bring you here?'

'I've got the information you wanted, about your father's place tomorrow.'

'Gosh, is it Thursday Ritual time again? Who's taking part this week?'

'So far? Team 1, Sam McNab the Undertaker with Pete Green and the Pallbearers; Team 2, old hands the Kelly Boys with their nasty little brother Joey K as decoy; Team 3, Mike Smith with Smiley Winters and PC Tanner; Team 4, Matt Holst and One Eyed Jed; Team 5, newcomers to the field, the Reverend Paul Oldham and his housekeeper Miss Hanson. And, as it's the second full week in the month, teams 6 and 7, The Parish Council and the WI.'

'Well done, Miss Susy. You're a real pearler!'

'It's not final, mind. They're all jockeying for position at the moment. I'll confirm the list of runners later, after closing time.'

'Great. Ready to give the interim report to Dad?'

Susy giggled. 'Of course. But is your old man ready to see me?'

She stood up, lifting her short skirt as if to retrieve her handkerchief. The manoeuvre revealed the top of her black stockings and a clip of her suspender belt.

'Phew! Miss Susy, don't do that up there. You'll give him a heart attack!'

'I was only finding my hankie; to dab that paint off your face.'

She licked a corner of the handkerchief and rubbed Freddie's face with it until all traces of paint had gone. The noises he made told her he clearly enjoyed the experience.

'That's better, Freddy. The things I do for you! Come on, let's see how far your old man's got with his Wednesday Checklist.'

A gentle breeze blew through the treetops as Freddie and Susy walked up the curved shingle avenue towards the main house. Birds sang sweetly around them and to their left, the sun flamed the clouds as it dipped towards the horizon.

'What a beautiful sunset,' Freddie remarked, calculating the paint colours needed to capture the fiery glow.

'So romantic,' said Susy, imagining a different picture. 'It's just the sort of night for a young man to go down on one knee to his sweetheart.'

Freddie was oblivious to the trap Susy was setting for him.

'Why should he do that?'

'You know,' she said, giggling.

'No.'

'Oh, Freddie!' she exclaimed, losing her patience. 'When are you going to make an honest woman of me?'

'What do you mean? You're not dishonest, are you?'

'You know very well what I mean, Freddie! They call me nasty things on the village. But if you were to, well, make me your intended, maybe that would stop.'

He felt her fingers walking up his arm again and became deliberately obtuse.

'I've never heard anyone calling you nasty things, Miss Susy. They're all very nice.'

'Sure, like the village bike!'

'There, see? That's nice.'

'No, it's not, Freddie! Don't you want someone to clean your home and cook your meals and wash your clothes and hang your pictures?'

'Yes, but I can't afford a housekeeper like Miss Hanson.'

'I'd be your housekeeper for nothing, if you married me.'

'That's a lovely offer, Miss Susy. But marriage is a serious step. Don't you think we're a little young?'

'But you're thirty-six. And I'm… old enough. I don't think you want to settle down at all.'

'You could be right, there.'

She burst into tears and lifted her skirt to retrieve her handkerchief from her stocking top again.

'After all I've done for you, Freddie! I'll end up a fat old battle axe, like Miss Hanson! And I thought you cared!'

Her show of emotion flustered him, just as she had intended.

'Miss Susy, please stop. I can't bear to see you like this!'

Her tears stopped at once.

'Then marry me, Freddie.'

'How can I marry you, Miss Susy? Father wouldn't approve.'

'Your father doesn't even know,' she wailed. 'You've just been leading me on, haven't you, Freddie? All that talk of yours about everyone being equal is just a con, isn't it? You never wanted me: you just wanted my information.'

'That's not true, Miss Susy! You know I've wanted several other things of yours too.'

'Really? Then whistle for them. I'm going to find me a real man!'

She turned and marched off back down the drive towards the Gatehouse, sobbing. He chased after her.

'Susan, stop! What about tomorrow? My parents are depending on you.'

'I don't want your parents. I want you. That's what I do all this for. So if you don't want me, they can whistle for it too!'

She pulled away from him and marched off towards the Gatehouse. He caught up with her and grabbed her arm to turn her around.

'Susan, please don't go. I don't know what I'd do without you.'

She stopped sobbing and blew her nose. At last she could deliver the ultimatum she had been trying to create. She looked him squarely in the eye.

'Then make me a convincing offer. Or never see me again.'

Freddie saw from her expression that she meant business. He breathed in deeply and gave her a conditional answer he thought she would never achieve.

'All right, Susan. If you manage to stop the Thursday Ritual, I'll marry you.'

She grabbed both his arms in delight.

'Thank you, Freddie! And when I do, I will accept.'

'But Susy, that's impossible!'

'Nothing's impossible,' she replied, and sealed the deal with a kiss.

The Gatehouse

Chapter 2: Planning and Preparation

2 : 1

The church clock struck seven thirty. For half an hour, the village of Little Piddlington hushed as its inhabitants paused from their daily round to watch Coronation Street. The only activity was at Lodge Castle, where Freddie's father Phil Farley took a break from his Wednesday Checklist to polish his heirlooms in the hall.

Pride of place in Phil's collection was given to a suit of armour much loved by his great-great-grandfather, Lord Montague Smithson Farley the Ninth. Phil looked uncommonly like the portrait of his favourite forebear which hung on the panelled staircase. Phil was tall, weedy and had a jutting pugnacious chin which just begged to be punched. His collar-length hair was Brilcreemed into place and his well-pressed trousers and 'County' style jumper were appropriate for his fancied place in society.

Unlike Phil, his favourite forebear Monty Farley Nine was an irascible eccentric who had owned much of the Black Country but spent his days jousting with those new-fangled railway engines. Surprisingly, Monty Farley Nine did not turn his toes up through multiple mediaeval injuries. He drank himself and his fortune to death because he had a secret guilt complex about owning mines. After his many embarrassing peccadillos came to light, the family lost its title, all its investments and most of its lands.

Phil took down the close helm steel helmet from Monty Farley

Nine's suit of armour and gave it a loving polish.

'Ah, Monty. When I put on this helmet of yours, my heart fills with ancestral pride.'

He slid the helmet over his head. The stiff helm clattered down, distorting his voice as he continued to speak.

'Or is it just the neck guard blocking the blood supply?'

The heavy oak front door creaked open and Freddie entered with Miss Susy. Her high-heeled shoes clip-clopped over the tiled chequerboard floor.

'Hello, Mr Farley,' she greeted. 'We've got some wonderful news to tell you.'

Her right foot hovered over a white tile.

'Not that tile! The black ones,' shouted Freddie, before she could trigger the trap his father would have set as part of the Wednesday Checklist.

'Hello, Freddie, Miss Sharp,' said Phil's distorted voice. 'Oh, dear. I can't seem to raise this visor.'

'What, Dad?'

'I said, I can't raise the visor!'

'We can't hear you, Dad.'

'The visor's stuck!' Phil said, pointing to the helmet.

'I think the visor's stuck,' squeaked Miss Susy: 'Let me help you, Mr Farley. If we could pull the helmet off.'

'What? I can't hear you.'

'Jut helping you pull it off.'

She wrapped her left leg around his thighs and tried to tug the helmet upwards.

'What?' said Phil. 'Oh, my goodness! What are your legs doing there?'

Freddie saw the helmet move a little through Susy's efforts.

'Move over, Miss Susy: let me get a hold,' he said. 'You count and I'll pull. Ready, Dad?'

'One,' cried Susy.

Freddie grunted and tugged at the helmet.

'Two!'

Grunt.

'Three!'

Grunt.

The Brilcreem-lubricated steel helmet flew off Phil's head and bounded across the floor, smashing the glass in a display cabinet of spurs. Phil staggered back onto a rusty lever. This released a heavy weight from the ceiling: the weight almost landed on top of him. Freddie staggered backwards and fell through a trapdoor into a pit of baying dogs. Fortunately, the dogs knew him well and tried to lick him into submission. En route, he shoved Miss Susy back. She collided with a suit of armour and fell through a false wall, to land in the basement, in the middle of the stream that had once saved the Farley family during a siege. The suit of armour collapsed onto the floor, shedding its round shield. The shield spun on its outer edge for several seconds, slowly losing momentum. It landed boss side up with a crash like a cymbal.

Phil gazed around the empty hall, puzzled and dazed. It looked as if it had just been the scene of a riot.

'They didn't stop long,' he said. Then he realised something was missing.

'And they took my helmet!'

The grandfather clock beside him whirred into life and rang in eight o'clock.

2 : 2

Eight o'clock was rung in by time-pieces all across the village, from the small Geneve chiming LCD watch on shopkeeper Sharkie Sharp's wrist to the big square-faced clock on the church tower. As the last bars of music closed the evening's episode of Coronation Street, housewives switched on kettles and publican Tom Oddfellow pulled pints again. The noise in the Saloon Bar swelled with the usual pub crowd debate over the latest plot twists. Outside, the evening calm was disturbed by the sound of an S&D dustcart heading up the lane towards the village from the main road.

The dustcart drew up and parked by the green opposite the pub. Pat Sewell jumped down from the driver's door, his hobnail boots thudding on the asphalt. He was a large, shadowy, muscular figure in the evening light, and was still wearing his pungent work clothes. He took a pocket watch out of his coarse waistcoat and checked it against the church clock.

'Eight o'clock. They should be far enough gone by now.'

He walked across the car park to the King's Arms and opened the door to the saloon bar. The noisy pub crowd fell instantly silent. Pete Green got up from his table and walked up to the stranger. He stopped inches away from him, his manner threatening as he blocked him from entering the bar.

'You're early, ain't you. Bin day's tomorrow,' Pete said.

The dustman mirrored his hostility.

'I'm not here collecting for the Council.'

PC Tanner crossed the bar to stand with Pete Green.

'Really, sir? Then why did you come in a refuse wagon?'

'How else was I to get to the village? You haven't had a bus in four years. They won't miss the old Sid and Dick overnight, and she'll be back in the Council depot by morning.'

'I see. Misappropriation of Council property,' said PC Tanner. He pulled out his off-duty notebook and pencil.

'It's all in a good cause,' Pat Sewell said: 'I represent the Up Effingham Morris Men. We're doing a sponsored Morris Dance tomorrow, and we'll be coming through here.'

The pub crowd exchanged knowing looks. The village was at the end of a road to nowhere. No-one ever just came through there, not even a sponsored Morris team.

Michelle 'Mike' Smith crossed the bar to join the confrontation at the door, her leathers gleaming in the saloon lights.

'I'll take over, PC Tanner,' she said.

'Fine, Mike. Just don't go too far,' he replied.

He stepped back with Pete Green to give Mike free range.

'Over here, stranger,' Mike said, gesturing an invitation to the dustman to join her at the corner table.

'Why should I, woman?' Pat Sewell sneered, even more confident when facing a member of the weaker sex.

'Don't be a fool, man. Nobody talks to Mike Smith that way,' warned publican Tom Oddfellow from the bar.

Pat Sewell stepped up close to Mike to crowd her the way Pete Green had crowded him.

'Transvestite, are you, Smith? You don't scare me none.'

'Sure, stranger; what if I am? What's your drink?'

'A pint, punk.'

'A pint for the stranger, Tom.'

PC Tanner threw some coins on the counter to cover her order.

'Coming right up,' Tom replied. As he pulled the pint, he warned, 'Don't do anything foolish, Mister. Remember, this is my bar.'

'Shut it, Tom!' Mike ordered.

Tom placed the brimming pint glass on the counter. Tanner gave it to Mike. She handed it to Pat, who took it in his right hand.

'Cheers, stranger,' Mike said.

'Cheers, Smith,' Pat replied.

As he raised the pint glass to his lips, Mike punched him in the stomach. He doubled up and dropped his glass. She struck his exposed neck with a karate chop and felled him. The pub crowd laughed mercilessly as he dropped on the floor.

After a few moments, he rolled over, dazed and groaning.

'What d'you do that for, Smith?' he gasped.

'We don't like strangers here, stranger,' she replied. 'Pete, Smiley, throw this refuse where it belongs.'

Pete Green and Smiley Winters leapt to obey. They dragged Pat Sewel out of the pub and across the road.

'No, not the dustcart! I'll be crushed to death!' Pat cried.

They ignored his protests and threw him into the back of his dustcart. Job done, they returned to the saloon bar, shutting the outside door on him. The pub crowd congratulated them. Conversation started up again in the bar.

'Well done, Mike. Another drink?' offered PC Tanner.

'Wouldn't say no, PC Tanner,' she replied.

'Same again, Tom,' Tanner ordered.

'Coming right up!' Tom said.

He pressed two spirit glasses against the whisky optic and handed them to them. They took their drinks over to Mike's corner table.

'You know, Mike, you ought to think of joining up,' Tanner said.

'What, the Police? I've already tried. After all, what other jobs are there here? Except the Forces; and killing people's against my conscience.'

'Did you get an interview?'

'Sure, and with a couple of forged references from Chief Constable Anderton and Willie Whitelaw, I thought I was well in. But no. They said I was too short.'

'So they did ask you to take your boots off!'

She frowned and looked across at him.

'How d'you know about that?'

2 : 3

Meanwhile, in the Snug Bar of the King's Arms, five local residents had gathered for the Piddlington Parish Council meeting. The wood-panelled Snug Bar was smaller than the saloon. Its battered square tables had been placed together to form a larger workspace, with the hard chairs gathered around, so that the Councillors could face each other and spread out their papers during the session. A serving hatch to the bar was shut, but it only took a quick knock for publican Tom Oddfellow to open the hatch and refill an empty glass.

The Council had gathered for its regular monthly debate about perennial local problems. Under Chairman Ted Banner's practised guidance, it was rediscovering its usual lack of decisions. Ted was a well-fed, red-faced man with a pugnacious sneer. He looked like the union leader Arthur Scargill and had a similar donkey jacket and flat cap dress sense, but a diametrically opposite philosophy of life.

'So you're all agreed with me: we leave the matter of china fly-tipping down by One Eyed Jed's caravan in Pond Spinney till the next meeting,' he said.

The four Parish Council members present all nodded and said "yes". To his right sat Mr Blake, lean, ferret-like and resolute, dressed in his well-worn best 1970s suit with the flared trousers and broad collars that used to be fashionable. By Mr Blake sat Major Harty: ramrod straight, smart in country casuals: a tan suede jacket and matching twill trousers. Opposite them sat Sharkie Shark: casually dressed and with a lean hunched look as if he was always hiding a lit cigarette or sneaking round a partly open door. The last member was Farmer Duncan, red-faced and bucolic, still dressed in the well-loved tweed jacket and trousers he had worn for milking.

'As time is short, gentlemen,' said Banner; 'I suggest we ask our Community Action Sub-Committee to look into item five, the issue of the poor of the village. Major Harty can report back to us on behalf of the Sub-Committee at the next meeting.'

The others nodded. Banner moved down the agenda to the next item, jotting notes as he went so that he could write up the minutes afterwards. He believed in running the Parish Council on a need-to-know basis. Major Harty heartily approved.

'Now, the problem of dogs fouling the footpath again,' Banner said: 'We've received another letter from Mrs Blake. Mr Blake, would you like to fill us in?'

'I would, Mr Chairman,' Gary Blake agreed earnestly. 'It's about time we found a real solution to this problem. We've discussed these dogs every meeting for the last thirty years.'

'Not the same dogs,' remarked Farmer Duncan.

Gary Blake thumped the table with his fist.

'That's just the sort of snide comment I've come to expect from you, Farmer Duncan. But I tell you, Mrs Blake's design for a canine convenience is the only effective answer. And my brother's building business has given a most competitive quote for the erection. Remember, these droppings are a health hazard. We've got to stamp it out once and for all!'

Farmer Duncan, Sharkie Sharp and Major Harty covered their faces to snigger at his verbal gaffe.

'We'll leave you to stamp on the problem, Mr Blake,' said Ted Banner. 'May I suggest a less unpleasant answer: writing threatening letters to the dog owners once again. Yes, Mr Sharp?'

'They don't heed our threats, Mr Chairman,' Sharkie Sharp replied. He sounded more like a spiv than a representative of the people. 'I hear them in my village store. "I got another letter from Ted Banner." "So did I. Let's report the Parish Council to the RSPCA!"'

'But if we can't stop the dogs, how will we stop the cows?' demanded Mr Blake.

'What're you accusing my cows of now, Mr Blake?' demanded Farmer Duncan.

'It's not your Jerseys, Farmer Duncan: it's those filthy Friesians from across the road,' Gary Blake replied.

'Them Friesians be my cows too, Mr Blake! And I'll trouble those that's unemployed like yourself not to criticise those what works hard for to earn their daily bread.'

'I object, Farmer Duncan! Clerk, strike that off the record. I'm not unemployed: I get very long holidays.'

'Arr, Mr Blake – all of two years so far.'

'You looking for trouble?'

Farmer Duncan and Gary Blake rose to face up to each other. Their staring match turned to blows. Sharkie Sharp and Major Harty cheered them on from the sidelines.

'Two to one on Duncan scoring the knockout blow,' Sharkie Shark offered as odds.

Ted Banner's calls for order went unnoticed. He tried a fresh approach and hit his empty glass with his pipe. The glass rang like a bell.

'End of Round One!' he called.

Blake stopped defending himself. Duncan threw one last lucky punch at the open target. Blake caught the blow on his chin. He flopped into his seat, his limbs no longer obeying him. Duncan strutted back round the table and to his place opposite him.

'Thank you, gentlemen!' Ted Banner reproved with a sneer. 'Now that I have your attention again, let's get back to the matter in hand: dogs fouling the footpaths. Mr Sharp is right to point out that our threatening letters are not threatening enough. Suggestions please, for more threatening threats from the floor...'

Blake duly slid from his seat and landed with a dazed thud on the grubby beige lino-covered floor.

'Mr Blake, what are you doing on your back?' Ted Banner asked.

'You did say *from the floor,*' he replied, still groggy from Farmer Duncan's last punch. 'How about a hundred pound fine?'

'Ineffective. Only landlord Tom Oddfellow can find that sort of money out of his own pocket these days. Major Harty?'

'Court martial 'em, what!'

'Alas, none of our villagers are members of the forces, more's the pity. Farmer Duncan?'

'Send Smiley Winters round to duff 'em up.'

'A little too heavy-handed at this stage. Mr Sharp?'

'We could, er, employ a teenager on Job Creation to shovel the dog dirt through the culprits' letter boxes.'

The other Councillors stared at him in surprise at such a novel idea. At first, they thought he had made a joke. On reflection, they saw the possible merits and applauded him. Gary Blake hauled himself back up off the floor onto his chair and clapped with them.

'Oh, excellent!' said Ted Banner: 'Not only effective, but it would create a job too. I propose a vote on the issue.'

'Seconded!' barked Major Harty.

'All those in favour of stamping on the problem with Mr Blake... None. All those in favour of easing the village unemployment problem with Mr Sharp's solution? Unanimous! Clerk, put an advert in tomorrow's Evening Packet for a community postman.'

Ted Banner paused to write a note instructing himself to place the advert. Though being both Clerk and Chairman had its drawbacks, it did also mean he had complete control.

'And now, our last item on the agenda, AOB,' Ted Banner announced: 'Clerk, this item is off the record. The Chair recognises Major Harty of the Community Action Sub-Committee.'

Major Harty stood up and bowed to Ted Banner.

'Thank you, Chairman. Yes, men, it's Lodge Castle time again. Now, when I was fighting the Burma Campaign...'

'Not the Burma Campaign again,' muttered Sharkie Sharp.

'Quiet, that man!' ordered Major Harty. 'Now, where was I? Oh, yes, the Burma Campaign. We had to surround a village full of I-ties…'

'That means it wasn't Burma, it was Italy,' said Mr Blake, leaning forward with his elbows on the table to steady himself.

'What? Italy, yes: just testing you. So these A-rabs dressed in curtains and what…'

'In Italy?' asked Farmer Duncan.

'No, that was Alexandria. So we surrounded the Schloss…'

'In Alexandria?' asked Sharkie Sharp.

'Stop heckling, Councillors, or we'll be here all night,' ordered Ted Banner. 'Major Harty, if we could perhaps move on from denigrating half the world's population and all our present allies, and get to the plan itself?'

'What? The plan. Yes. From my considerable wartime experience, it was quite clear to me why we have to date been unsuccessful in our campaign. An unauthorised person has been listening in.'

'What?' said Ted Banner.

'It's catching,' remarked Mr Blake.

'Sharkie Sharp, check the window,' Ted Banner ordered; 'Farmer Duncan, the door!'

Feet clattered across the lino floor. Sharkie Sharp pulled up the sash cord window and brought it back down on Joey K's fingers. The boy howled with pain and fell backwards into the flower bed outside.

Farmer Duncan threw open the Snug Bar door. He revealed Pete Green crouching in the hall with his ear at keyhole level.

'Oh, er, hello, Farmer Duncan,' Pete Green said, straightening.

'Goodbye, Pete Green,' Farmer Duncan replied, and landed a

well-placed punch in his solar plexus. Pete cried out and fell to the floor, clutching his stomach.

Sharkie Sharp and Farmer Duncan returned to their seats. They turned their attention back to the meeting as if nothing untoward had happened.

'Thank you, gentlemen,' said Ted Banner. 'Is that better, Major Harty?'

'Yes. But we can't take any chances. So this month, I'm not going to tell you about our plan.'

'Most laudable, Major. But if you don't tell us what it is, how can we carry it out?' Ted Banner asked.

'I'll come to that shortly,' the Major replied. 'Now, we all know the obstacles: broken glass on the wall, electric perimeter fence, only entrance booby-trapped, trenches bordering the drive, plus the three starving Alsatians, the tip-beam across the well, the barbed wired kitchen garden, the suspended flowerpots in the potting shed. Not to mention the courtyard cobbles wired to an automatic rifle. And that's just the grounds.'

'As we have all discovered,' said Ted Banner. 'How do you propose we should deal with them? Or aren't you going to tell us that either?'

'Ah, Chairman. Now for my master stroke.'

Major Harty emptied the contents of a large envelope onto the battered table. Out tumbled four rice paper sheets, each folded into the shape of an envelope and individually addressed. He handed them out.

'In these rice paper envelopes are your instructions, Councillors. Read them, eat them, and inwardly digest.'

The men opened their envelopes and read their instructions. The doubt in their expressions turned into surprise and approval. They looked over the shoulders of the others to see their roles and gain an idea of the complete picture rather than just their part. Murmurs of approval were expressed.

'I think we're on to a winner this time. Well done, Major Harty,' said Ted Banner. 'Do you agree, Council?'

The members all raised their right hands in agreement. They passed the plan on the nod and ate their rice paper sheets. Once all traces of the plan had gone, Ted Banner shut the minute book in front of him.

'Gentlemen, I wish you all luck for tomorrow. There being no further business, I declare the meeting closed.'

2 : 4

Meanwhile, in the Lounge Bar of the King's Arms, the local Women's Institute group had gathered for its monthly exchange of facts and skills. The Lounge Bar benefitted from hard-wearing cushions on the solid wooden chairs, and newer tables with fewer dents and scratches on which to work. A blackboard stood in one corner, covered by a worn rose-patterned single sheet. The tables were covered in the paper and materials Mrs Mabel McNab had encouraged other members to use in her latest session of *A Hundred and One Ways to Arrange a Single Rose*. Mrs McNab was a portly and enthusiastic lady who loved demonstrating arts and crafts. She also loved to wear clothes of her own creation in wool and flax dyed with colours she had made herself from local plants and insects. She regularly offered to run demonstrations for the local Brownies and

Guides and was just as regularly turned down because the local company Guider Mrs Jennifer Blake knew just how boring she could be.

'And with another piece of toilet paper, like so…' Mrs McNab continued. The toilet paper rustled and transformed in her hands. '…You can even make our symbol, WI!'

'Oh,' sighed the other members, sounding bored but also a little impressed. They gave the speaker a short round of half-hearted applause.

'And that's it for this month. Back to Mrs Harty.'

Their Chairwoman stood up as the speaker sat down. Mrs Gwendoline Harty looked like a female version of her husband, Major Harty. Her posture was ramrod straight, her steel-grey hair clipped in a neat short bob, her grey-green suit a civilian version of what she had worn in the army.

'Thank you, once again, Mrs McNab, for your interesting and informative talk about yet more ways to arrange a single rose. The hour simply sped by, didn't it, ladies?'

Mrs Banner, Mrs Duncan and Mrs Smith muttered as they gave a second half-hearted round of applause.

'Oh, yes!' agreed Mrs Rosie Banner with a wry grimace. She was an attractive grey-haired woman, smartly dressed in a navy blue twinset and pearls. It was a great disappointment to her as a trophy wife that her husband Ted Banner had not become Lord Lieutenant of the County in return for his decades of civic service leading the Parish Council.

'On square wheels,' said Mrs Maude Duncan. She looked the farmer's wife she was. Her weathered face was rosy-cheeked. She wore her long greying hair in an untidy bun and clothed her ample body in a well-washed floral print cotton dress under a hand-knitted amber cardigan.

'For a tortoise,' said Mrs Jane Smith. Her big hair and Dolly Parton style dress looked somewhat out of place among the rural fashions of the other members.

'Now, ladies: calm down,' ordered Mrs Harty. 'At last, the moment we've all been waiting for. Twenty-fourth in our monthly series, please welcome our village company Guider Mrs Blake, with *Practical Map Reading.*'

Mrs Jennifer Blake leapt to her feet, radiating enthusiasm. She was still wearing her mid-blue shirt dress and her sensible flat black brogues. An Alice band held back her shoulder-length blonde hair and her homely round face radiated energy.

The other members cheered and clapped her with equal enthusiasm as she moved the sheet-covered blackboard forward to a position where all could see it. When she was ready, she blew a sharp blast on her Guide whistle to stop the cheers.

'Really, girls! Control yourselves!' she ordered with an affectionate smile. 'Now, I expect you've all been wondering what I have hidden under this sheet.'

She picked up a corner of the sheet and whisked it off to one side, revealing a map of the locality drawn in smudged chalk.

'Yes, it's our old map of Lodge Castle, showing this month's winning scheme for assaulting the Post Office. The lucky contestant is Mrs Banner, who wins our everlasting box of groceries and, if her plan works, the cut glass rose bowl. Well done, Mrs Banner.'

Mrs Harty handed over a cellophane-wrapped box of out-of-date groceries to a bashful Mrs Banner amidst more applause.

'And now to business,' said Mrs Blake. 'This month we have a lot more information, thanks to the travelling bread van. The main point to watch is here, the entrance porch to the main house. The symbols depict a trip wire linked to a net-full of rock buns.'

'Child's play!' called out Mrs Smith.

'Rock buns? They won't harm us!' shouted Mrs Duncan.

'Ah, but these aren't ordinary rock buns, girls. We all know Mrs Farley's reputation as a cook. She may claim that Sharkie Sharp – sorry, Mrs Sharp – that Mr Sharp sold her old plaster instead of flour, but with the Vicar's jaw dislocated last week and Miss Hanson's false teeth broken, it's quite clear that they are really – her secret weapon!'

The other members expressed their surprise and horror. Mrs Smith booed.

'So what can we do about it?' continued Mrs Blake. 'This is where Mrs Banner's plan is so ingenious. Following our recent learning project, *Win a Pilot's Licence*, Mrs Banner has come up with the novel solution of flying in by helicopter – over the wall!'

Oohs and ahs came from the impressed members.

'Well done, Mrs Banner, and thanks for volunteering to fly the Sea King with me,' said Mrs Blake. 'Now, tomorrow's itinerary. At seven hundred hours, Party A will set off for RAF Much Muckleham to take up Commander Millet-Airey's kind invitation for us to have a flight in one of his helicopters. Once in flight, Party A will overcome the pilot and fly the Sea King over to Farmer Jones' black field to pick up Party B and our standard assault packs. We will then fly on to the Lodge Castle grounds and intercept the Post Office security van here, between the gateway and the house. We will winch the van off the ground and fly it over to Mrs Duncan's farm, where we will hide it in the pig byre until the security men are starved out or Mrs Smith has cut it open with her do-it-yourself oxyacetylene cutting gear. Any questions?'

Only Mrs Duncan put up her hand. 'Arr. What if the van is early?' she asked.

'Your own observations can answer that, Mrs Duncan. Of the 227 times we have logged the van's arrival, 51 times it was punctual, 176 times it was late, and never, ever, has it been early. No more questions? Then back to you, Mrs Harty.'

Mrs Blake pulled the rose-patterned sheet back over the blackboard. Mrs Harty stood up and handed out small cards to everyone present.

'Thank you, Mrs Blake. Ladies, these cards allocate your team divisions. Once again, best of luck. And remember, the name of the WI movement goes with us. Don't bring it into disrepute. We are meant to be good, clean-living village housewives; so no glimmer of intelligence from any of you! Company dismissed.'

2 : 5

Meanwhile, in the Snooker Room of the King's Arms, the Kelly boys were holding a more informal planning meeting while they potted the odd ball. The two lanky young men had hungry eyes and surly faces. Unemployed twenty-year-old Kev handled his snooker cue with the ease of a person who had spent a lot of time playing, while late teenager Keith was relatively new to the world of work and signing on. The snooker table they circled was the only item of furniture in the dingy wood-panelled room apart from some wooden benches around the walls. The sash cord window was bare, and a board blocked the serving hatch to the bar.

'Good shot, Kelly,' said Kev, as Keith's cue hit the cue ball and sent it across the snooker table to bounce off the cushion.

'Not good enough to beat you, Kelly,' Keith replied, watching Kev's shot sending the black ball into the corner pocket. 'There goes sooty.'

'Never mind, bruvver. You're getting better.'

'Gee, d'you really think so, Kelly?'

'I know so, bruv: it took me all of three minutes to beat you this time.'

'It helped when you explained about the holes.'

'Pockets, bruv, pockets. Another game?'

'Yes please, Kelly.'

Kev dropped some coins into the pay slot. The table released the balls for another game. He shaped the reds with the triangular wooden rack and played on as they continued to talk.

'Are you all set for tomorrow, Kelly?' asked Kev.

'Course I am, Kelly,' Keith replied.

'Only we don't want anything to happen like last week, do we?'

'How was I to know you'd got the steak to keep the Alsatians quiet? It made a nice tea, you must admit: better than baked beans again.'

'Lovely! It knocked us out for three days. Seventy-two hours of my love life wasted through your stupidity!'

'You're a right one to talk! What about you the week before: stuck down a blocked off chimney cos you forgot Phil Farley had had central heating put in.'

'How was I to know? He didn't ask us to instal it. He phoned a reputable fly-by-night firm.'

The door sprang open and bashed against the wall, revealing Mike Smith. Smiley Winters and PC Tanner flanked her. The racket from the crowd in the Saloon Bar filled the room. The Kelly boys stopped playing and moved to the other side of the snooker table for protection.

'Well, well, well, what have we here?' said Mike Smith. She had to shout above the racket to be heard.

'Excuse me, miss, but shouldn't that be my line?' PC Tanner asked her.

'Oh no. Not Mike Smith!' said Kev.

'And Smiley Winters and PC Tanner,' added Keith.

'Hello, Kelly,' said Smiley with a benign smile.

'Hello, hello, hello,' said PC Tanner, tapping his left palm with his truncheon.

'Shurrup, boys! Constable, close the door!' Mike ordered.

She stepped forward into the room, expecting her team to follow. The Snooker Room door slammed shut, leaving her alone inside with the Kelly boys. She opened the door again, a resigned look on her face.

'With you two on this side!'

'Sorry, Mike,' Tanner replied.

He entered the Snooker Room with Smiley Winters and closed the door again. The noise from the busy Saloon Bar receded. The Kelly brothers shook their heads and went back to their snooker game. Kev played a shot that went wide.

'Oi, Kelly boys! Stop playing when I wanna talk to you!' Mike ordered.

Keith hit the best shot he had ever played, and a red ball flew down a corner pocket.

'How was we to know, Mike? Hey, stop it, Kelly!' Kev ordered.

'But I've just made an ace shot, Kelly. I could even beat you!' Keith replied.

'So you could! I didn't realise,' Kev lied.

'Smiley, the cue!' Mike ordered.

'Right, Mike,' Smiley said, and went to stand behind PC Tanner.

'Not that sort of queue, Smiley: this sort!'

Mike grabbed Keith's snooker cue and handed it to him.

'Break it, Smiley. No, not over PC Tanner. Try your knee. No, don't try to break your knee…'

Smiley finally caught on and snapped the snooker cue in two.

'Kelly, they broke my cue!' Keith wailed.

'If you wanted to take it home, Mike, why didn't you just unscrew it?' Kev asked.

'Cos I didn't come here for a snooker cue, Kelly.'

'So, what did you come here for?' asked Keith.

'Don't ask things like that,' Kev warned.

'For you, Kelly,' Mike replied, pointing at Keith.

'Oh, Mike! A girlfriend at last! I'm honoured.'

'Believe that too long, you'll also be dead!' Mike warned.

'Yeah, dead,' Smiley repeated.

He wrapped his arms around Keith's chest and lifted him off the floor. Keith struggled against the powerful grip but could not break his hold. He resorted to crying to Kev for help.

'Smiley, put my little bruvver down!' Kev said tiredly: 'Mike, keep your muscle-bound parrot under control.'

Smiley dropped Keith. He landed with a thud, on his backside on the floor.

'And you can shut it too, Kelly,' Mike warned: 'Unless you want PC Tanner to do you for the lead you stripped off the church roof.'

'How d'you know about that, Mike?'

'Your obnoxious little brother Joey K doesn't always keep things in the family. He'll do anything for a new catapult or a penny whistle.'

'So that's where he gets them,' Tanner said: 'I could open a toyshop with what I've confiscated from that lad.'

'Shut it, Tanner, or you may have to,' Mike warned.

'Ha, ha, ha: you ain't got nothing on me, Mike,' Tanner laughed.

'No? What was your panda car doing all steamed up last night in Pond Spinney?'

'Just escaped from the zoo?' quipped Keith.

Smiley grabbed his left arm and pulled it up behind his back.

'Ow! Only joking, Smiley. Leave go of my arm.'

Mike nodded. Smiley released him. Keith pulled away and nursed his sore arm, whimpering softly. Mike saw from the men's faces that she had softened them all up enough to move on to the next stage.

'Fine, gents. Now to business. Joey K tells me you Kelly boys are using him as a decoy tomorrow, while you have a go at the Post Office.'

'I'll murder that little brat!' Kev muttered.

'Don't be too hasty – it might do you good. Cos my team's gonna join you.'

'But that means we'll only get half the cash,' Keith objected.

'It means you'd succeed where you'd fail on your own. In this room, we've got all the meanest, dirtiest crooks in Little

64

Piddlington.'

'I did have a bath last week,' Keith remarked.

'Shut it, Kelly,' Kev hissed.

'If we work against each other, we're bound to fail,' Mike said; 'But together? Nothing can stand in our way, especially with the police turning a blind eye.'

'I'll be borrowing One Eyed Jed's spare eye patch,' Tanner said. 'What d'you say, boys?'

'I'd say, we haven't much choice, Mike,' Kev replied. 'What's your plan?'

'My plan is, we all follow your plan, Kelly.'

'Then I should get half the proceeds for thinking up the plan,' Kev said.

Smiley wrapped his arms around Kev's chest. He lifted him bodily off the floor, crushing his chest until he pleaded to be put down. The point made, Smiley dropped him on the floor.

'What *is* your plan, Kelly?' Mike asked.

'You tell 'em, Kelly,' Kev gasped.

'And have you blame me for splitting on us, Kelly? Not likely!'

'The plan, Kelly!' Mike ordered.

'All right, all right,' Kev panted. He leaned over the snooker table for support. 'Pretend this table is the Lodge Castle grounds. The cushion is the outer wall. The far end's the kitchen garden. This line of chalk cubes is the drive. I'll move these balls to represent the house.'

'Hey, that's my winning game!' Keith objected.

Smiley growled at him and caught hold of his collar.

'Only joking, Smiley,' Keith backed down, and thanked him when he let him go again.

Kev arranged the red balls into a square and replaced one of the reds with the yellow. He had given all the coloured balls nicknames.

'This yellow ball, Primrose, is the Post Office, beside the study and the hall.'

'Fine. Now tell us something we don't know,' Mike said.

'Patience, Mike: I'm getting to it.'

'You're wasting valuable drinking time, too. Tanner, get in the drinks – it's your round.'

'It's always my round.'

Despite his protest, Tanner knocked on the wooden hatch. Tom Oddfellow opened it and took his order for the usual for everyone. The gang waited until their drinks were in their hands and the hatch had closed again, before they resumed their discussion around the improvised map.

'Right. We'll be getting into the grounds here: a quick pole-vault over the wall,' Kev said, patting the cushion near the end representing the orchard.

'Will we? And what will we land on?' Mike asked in disbelief.

'All thought of,' Kev replied. 'Young Kelly here'll've come round a bit earlier with Farmer Duncan's hay wain. He'll leave it on this side of the wall for us to land on.'

'Right. Smiley'll go with you, Kelly, to make sure you leave the hay wain in the right place.'

'Oh. Lovely,' Keith said, not impressed.

'Wouldn't it be better if we all hid in the hay wain? Then Keith and Smiley can drive us all in,' said Tanner.

'Afraid of heights, PC Tanner?' Mike taunted.

'It's not that. I just can't pole-vault over eight foot, and that wall's easily ten foot not counting the glass.'

'Good point, Constable: my own personal best is about nine foot three,' Kev said. 'So we all come in the hay wain, with Joey K. On my signal, he'll dash into the house to create a diversion with his catapult.'

'I'd better return it to him, then,' said Tanner.

'Then we'll all dash in, take 'em by surprise, snatch the loot and make our getaway.'

'In the hay wain?' asked Mike.

'How about my panda car?' suggested Tanner: 'That wouldn't look strange outside the Post Office on a Thursday. It might even keep the other raiders away.'

'Even better, we could all come in the panda car,' said Kev; 'How many d'you think you could hide in the boot?'

The Kelly boys and Mike Smith's team worked on late into the evening.

2 : 6

As darkness filled the valley with shadows, the village of Little Piddlington settled for the night. Before the church clock struck 10.30, the WI ladies had already tucked themselves up in bed to be ready for their early morning start. The Parish Council members soon followed. At picturesque thatched Lilac Cottage, Chairman Ted Banner quietly closed his front door and paused in the hall. The sound of snoring came from the main bedroom.

Ted crept up the creaking stairs and opened the bedroom door. His wife snorted in her sleep and turned over. Silence returned to the bedroom, but for the ticking of the alarm clock. Ted switched on the light, sat on the bed and took off his boots, dropping them on the floor with a thud. Mrs Banner woke up with a start.

'You're in bed early, dear,' said Ted, his voice wheedling.

'Humph!' his wife replied. She rolled over in the bedclothes to turn her back on him.

'I know you're awake, Rosie,' he whispered, leaning over where he thought her ear would be.

'I wasn't till you came in, Ted.'

She sat up, yawned, and looked at the clock standing by the book on the bedside cabinet beside her. Then she remembered why he was late and wondered if she could persuade him to let slip some details of the Parish Council's Post Office plan.

'How did your meeting go?' she asked.

'Very well, dear. Our new Community Action Programme looks very promising. How did your meeting go?'

'Very well, too, dear. Practical Map Reading again, and I won the box of everlasting groceries. I'll have to give it back, of course, for next month's prize.'

He slid into bed beside her.

'Well done, dear. You'll be feeling in a good mood, then, eh? Eh?' he said and caressed her cheek.

'Stop it, Ted. I've got a headache!' she ordered.

She flung her bedside book at him. It hit his head with a thud and fell to the floor.

'Ouch! Suddenly, so have I!'

Meanwhile, in the village store across the green, Councillor Sharkie Sharp was still hard at work, pricing up the products delivered earlier that day. The village shop was the sort of store that seemed to sell everything. So many products were on display, only three customers could stand in the shop at any one time. Sharkie pulled a heavy cardboard box towards him across the heavy wooden counter and opened out the flaps.

'And best EEC mountain butter? Yes, give 'em a bargain.'

His black permanent marker squeaked across a bright yellow cardboard price tag.

'49 pence a packet: today's bargain, 99 pence for two.'

The street door opened and the bell jangled. Miss Susy clip-clopped in on her teetering high heel shoes. She shut the door behind her.

'Hi, Daddy. Good meeting?' she asked.

She sounded preoccupied, which was unusual for her. He looked at her face in concern.

'Susan, what are you doing home so early?' he asked.

'I need your advice, Daddy.'

He came out from behind the counter and put his arm around her shoulders.

'Are you all right, baby doll? You aren't – you know…'

'Oh, no, Daddy: nothing like that. Freddie Farley's finally said he'll marry me.'

'But that's wonderful news, Susan. When's the happy day?'

'That's the problem. He said he'll only marry me when I stop the Thursday Ritual. He thinks that's impossible. I told him, nothing's impossible. But when I started thinking about it, I realised he's right.'

'Nonsense, Susan: there's always a way.' Sharkie thought quickly and recalled a conversation in the shop. 'Why, Mrs Farley said only yesterday, while she was getting some more baking plaster; if Lodge Castle gets robbed once more, they'll give up the Post

Office.'

'Give it up? But that's awful!'

'Not when I'm about to sign a contract to become a branch of the Somerset Central Bank. Only keep that under your hat for now.'

He tapped his nose with his right forefinger to emphasise the need for secrecy.

'Of course, Daddy. So what you're saying is, if the Post Office gets done again, the Farleys will give it up, and the Thursday Ritual will disappear.'

'That's it, baby doll.'

'But how can I raid the Post Office? No-one's managed to do it once this year.'

'Oh, no; you shouldn't take the money. You need to look loyal to the Farleys.'

She thought about this. The penny quickly dropped.

'Oh, I see what you mean, Daddy: then Phil and Anne Farley will be more likely to give us their consent. But I still don't think that will happen.'

'Don't you worry about Phil and Anne: when the time comes, I'll deal with them. Now, the reason no-one manages to do over the Post Office, is that we all get in each other's way. So all you have to do is stop every team from getting through but one.'

She thought about this. Understanding soon dawned.

'Of course, Daddy! But which one do I let through?'

'The team with the best plan, obviously: the Parish Council.'

Susy's face brightened as she saw her hopes for a better life finally coming within her grasp.

They quickly put away the last of the new stock and retired to the back room to discuss how she might pull it off.

2 : 7

Meanwhile, next door in the King's Arms, publican Tom Oddfellow was closing up for the night. He called last orders at twenty past ten and pulled down the metal grill over the bar at precisely 10.30 pm. After the ten minutes drinking up time was over, he started trying to winkle the noisy bunch of inebriates he called his customers, outside.

'Let's be having you, gentlemen. Haven't you got homes to go to?'

Someone pushed open the Saloon Bar door and the pub crowd staggered out into the night, telling each other to be quiet at the tops of their voices as the village would be asleep. He followed the last of them to bolt the swing doors and saw Jack Smith stagger to the right, heading for the Vicarage. Pete Green noticed him too.

'Hey, not that way, Jack!' he called.

Jack lurched through a turn and headed back towards The Cottages.

'Thanks, Pete: forgot where home was for a minute,' he replied, his words indistinct.

'See you tomorrow, eight-thirty sharp, for Mrs Holst's funeral,' Pete reminded him.

'Hey, Pete, take Dave with you,' Tom Oddfellow called.

Pete could not recall seeing his fellow pallbearer Dave Tripp since that evening's episode of Coronation Street.

'Dave? He left a couple of hours ago,' he said back.

'Only his senses. You'll find him under table two.'

Pete came back and helped Tom drag Dave out from under the

table. As Pete guided Dave back to his home at number 5, The Cottages, Tom closed and bolted the Saloon Bar door behind them.

'At least they aren't hard to throw out at closing time,' he said.

He went behind the bar to check the till. His takings were up again, despite running out of home-brew. Wednesdays were always a good night, and Thursdays too.

'Just as well they don't realise I take as much each week as the Post Office gets. Better check the rooms.'

He opened the Snug Bar door and looked inside. It looked as if a football team had changed there, not the Parish Council.

'What a mess! I should stop letting the Council use the Snug.'

He shut the door again, leaving the mess for pub cleaner Mrs Green to sort in the morning, and walked along the passage to the Lounge Bar at the back of the pub. When he opened that door, he sighed to see the tables and floor covered in snippets of tissue paper and cloth.

'And the WI are even worse. Mrs McNab's *Hundred and one ways to arrange a single rose* again.'

He switched off the light, shut the Lounge Bar door, and walked back along the passage to the Snooker Room. As he opened the door, Kev Kelly placed a black snooker ball on the table. It was clear he and the others were well worse for wear with the drink.

'But you said sooty was the Post Office, Kelly,' Mike Smith complained.

'The pink ball is the getaway vehicle,' added PC Tanner.

'Oh, yeah, Constable. So it won't be parked in the hall,' Kev said.

'You wouldn't get it through the front door, Kelly,' said Keith. 'Even Smiley knows that.'

'Do I, Mike?' Smiley Winters asked her.

'You do now, Smiley,' she replied.

'You lot, haven't you got homes to go to,' Tom interrupted.

'Oh, our friendly neighbourhood publican,' sneered Mike. 'You been listening in, Oddfellow?'

'I wouldn't have learnt much if I had. Are you about finished in here?'

'A few more minutes, Tom. Police business. You know,' said Tanner.

'All right, Constable. I'll bolt the serving hatch and lock all the doors. Give us a shout when you want out.'

Tom nodded to him and closed the Snooker Room door. After he had locked up the pub for the night, he washed up the last of the glasses in the scullery. The thick security glass in the scullery window blazed with a light burning at the neighbouring Vicarage. He put the glasses away and went to bed, wondering what kept the Vicar up so late.

2 : 8

The lights burned late in the Vicarage as the Vicar tussled with his conscience. His housekeeper Emily Hanson was supporting him in the chintzy lounge, by continually refreshing the tea trolley for him.

'More tea, Vicar?' she invited.

'I wish you would stop saying that, Miss Hanson. I shall be running all night,' the Vicar replied.

'As long as you're in the running tomorrow,' she giggled.

'I don't know, Miss Hanson. It sounds far more dangerous than I thought.'

'Nothing will happen to you if you tell the truth.'

'Carrying a little box and saying I'm collecting for the Church Roof Restoration Fund is hardly telling the truth when I'm about to rob the Post Office. What about the eighth commandment?'

Miss Hanson tutted impatiently.

'Haven't you listened to a word I've said, Vicar? I'll be the one who takes the money. Your morals won't be compromised at all – you're only there to distract the Farleys' attention.'

'Perhaps. But still my conscience tells me it's not right.'

'Tell me one commandment that says you mustn't go collecting door to door while I collect safe to safe?'

The Vicar considered this. 'None springs to mind,' he said.

'And how else will we get the funds to repair the church roof? The appeal has run for a year so far, and all you've raised is a pound and threepence ha'penny the Kelly boys gave me when Mike Smith made Kevin Kelly admit to stealing the lead in the first place.'

'I suppose desperate straits do need desperate measures, Miss Hanson. What other problems will we face?'

'That's the spirit, Vicar. Have another cup of tea.'

She poured more tea and milk into a floral cup and handed it to him on its dainty matching saucer.

'Thank you, Miss Hanson. I'm all ears. And tea.'

Miss Hanson assumed her Sunday School Teacher persona as she continued their conversation.

'The Post Office is on the ground floor and used to be a music room. Above the door hangs a concealed portcullis poised to fall on an unwary intruder and impale him to the blood stain effect floor tiles.'

The Vicar shuddered. 'Please don't, Miss Hanson. I see myself impaled upon those tiles.'

'Nonsense, Vicar. Trust God. Daniel survived the lions' den.'

'Daniel wasn't out to rob a Post Office.'

She looked at him with her witheringly stern schoolteacher glare.

'You realise, of course, Vicar, that if you don't raise the roof money from the parish, the Diocese will take it out of your stipend.'

The Vicar paled and gulped a swallow.

'Carry on then, Miss Hanson.'

She smiled and returned to the lesson.

'The walls of the Post Office are booby-trapped with out-of-date fireworks confiscated when Sharkie Sharp and others tried to storm Lodge Castle last spring.'

'Not bangers? I don't like loud noises.'

'Then don't touch the walls. The fixed counter is made of stone, and behind the electrified wire grille stands a life-sized cut-out picture of Mr Farley, which Farmer Duncan shoots each week. And he says he doesn't need glasses!'

'So that's why I've buried thirteen Philip Farleys since I came here. I always wondered why no-one attends the funerals.'

'It makes a regular income for McNab's funeral parlour. The Post Office pays his bill, and he reuses the coffin each week.'

'Perhaps I should think of something like that for the church, if this fails.'

'It won't fail, Vicar. Not if you do exactly what I say.'

2 : 9

Meanwhile, on the far side of the church graveyard, lights also burned late at Lodge Castle as the Farleys locked up for the night.

'Power to counter grille?' called Mrs Anne Farley.

She was a wiry fifty-six-year-old woman with short, straight iron grey hair and a wry, thin-lipped smile. Her choice of clothing was always practical. For the countdown checklist, she always wore a trouser suit in dark blue serge.

The power switch to electrify the counter grill had been installed inside the Post Office by the counter door. Phil Farley opened the door and reached in to pull down the heavy lever.

'Power on,' he confirmed.

'Cannonade?'

He crossed the hall to the control box by the main door.

'Guns primed and ready.'

'Burglar alarm?'

'Alarm on.'

The couple heaved a sigh of relief.

'That's it, dear: our 237-item checklist completed once again,' said Anne.

'Yes, dear.' Phil yawned. 'Time for bed at last.'

Behind them, their tortoiseshell cat Beatrice, miaowed and scratched at the heavy wooden front door.

'Oh, no! Who forgot to put the cat out?' Phil said.

He started throwing back switches, unlocking doors and shifting heavy weights, knowing they would have to go through all the checklist again once Beatrice had gone out for the night.

2 : 10

By midnight, most of the inhabitants of Little Piddlington had settled for the night. The only people still up were the members of Mike Smith's team in the snooker room of the King's Arms. They continued to work on their plan far into the night.

All looked the worse for wear. Smiley Winters lay slumped in a corner of the bench, snoring. The others looked and sounded very tired. Mike's hand, when she placed the yellow ball back on the snooker table, was erratic.

'But Mike, Primrose is the post office, remember?' said PC Tanner. Kev had given all the colour balls special names halfway through the planning session, saying it would confuse eavesdroppers. It certainly confused the gang.

'Sorry, Constable. I forgot,' she replied.

Keith Kelly placed his cue on the table and made an erratic shot. The white cue ball dribbled slowly across the baize and knocked the yellow into a corner pocket.

'You stupid idiot, Kelly. That's the last ball gone,' Kev swore.

'Sorry, bruv,' Keith replied.

'Bash him, Smiley,' Mike ordered.

'Mmph? Later,' Smiley replied and fell back asleep.

'Anyone got change for the snooker table?' PC Tanner asked.

Keith dug deep in his pocket and inserted two ten pence pieces in the slot at one end of the table. The mechanism released the balls into the tray below. Tanner placed them back on the table.

'Right, this line of chalk is the house wall, this broken cue is the drive, and Primrose here is the post office. Back to you, Kelly,' said

Tanner.

'Thanks, Constable,' said Keith. 'So as I was saying, we escape out of Primrose, run past the broken cue, and make our getaway up the line of chalk to the cushion in the cue ball. Like so.'

Keith struck the cue ball and sent it bounding across the table to bounce off the far cushion and disappear down the far corner pocket.

'And that's my plan,' he concluded.

'Brill, Kelly. Never knew you had it in you, bruv,' said Kev.

'Then we're all agreed at last,' Mike sighed in relief.

'Yes. We follow Kelly's plan,' said Tanner.

Everyone else nodded, except for Smiley Winters.

'What?' he asked, his eyes glazed.

'Never mind, Smiley,' Mike said.

'What's the time?' asked Kev.

'Not quite a quarter to three,' Tanner said, looking at his watch.

'Hey, it's tomorrow already,' said Keith.

'We'd better get back home and grab some kip,' said Kev.

'Yeah. Meet up again at the phone box by the church in four hours,' ordered Mike.

Kev acknowledged her with a tired wave and walked towards the door.

'Four hours? What about my beauty sleep?' Keith complained.

'Smiley can always rearrange your face for you,' Mike replied.

'Yeah,' said Smiley, smiling at the prospect of carrying out that order.

'Hey, the door's locked. How do we get out of here?' Kev asked, rattling the door handle.

'Call the landlord?' Keith suggested.

'At this hour? I would 'ave to arrest you for disturbing the peace,' Tanner warned.

'How about the window?' Mike asked.

Keith crossed the room and tried the sash cord window. It would not budge.

'It's all jammed up with paint, Mike,' Keith said.

'Smiley, open the window for us,' Mike ordered.

'Sure, Mike,' he replied.

He grabbed hold of the window frame and wrenched it out of the wall. The sound as it came out, was deafening in the quiet of the night. A chilly breeze blew into the room. He placed the frame on the floor with a heavy thud.

'Thanks, Smiley,' Mike said: 'Nothing like a bit of breaking and exiting to start the day. After you, gentlemen.'

Kev left first. He jumped out through the window without looking and fell further than he had expected. His cry of surprise failed to warn the others.

Keith climbed through the window next and fell with a similar cry, landing on his brother. Smiley Winters followed him out and crushed them both. Smiley provided PC Tanner with a softer landing. Their yells as they fell and "oofs" as they landed, forewarned Mike. She looked down from the window at the untidy heap of bodies in the near-darkness.

'So there is a ten-foot drop outside this window.'

She jumped out and landed on top of them all. Kev tried to grab her, but she stood up too quickly and stepped back. With a wry smile, she dusted off her hands.

'Thanks for the soft landing, fellas. See you all in four hours.'

Her platform boots clomped awkwardly across the road and up the path to number 3, The Cottages. The front door was unlocked when she tried the handle. She saw the light in the back kitchen as she walked in and guessed her parents had waited up for her.

'Home, Mam. Home, Dad!' she called to them.

'And about time, too! Where have you been all night, eh? Your father and me have been worried sick, haven't we, Jack?' said Jane Smith.

'Mmm,' said Jack Smith.

They were seated at the back kitchen table. The tea pot and dirty cups in front of them told of an all-night sitting. Mike shook her head in disbelief.

'I was only over the Queen's Legs with PC Tanner and the rest. I'm hardly likely to come to any harm there,'

'True,' said Jack.

'It's not a matter of whether you come to any harm or not, Michelle: it's a matter of where you were, isn't it, Jack?'

'Is it? Oh, yes,' he said.

'But Mam, I told you where I was going, last night, before I left.'

'You said you were going to the Queen's Legs to see Smiley Winters. You didn't say nothing about PC Tanner. You could have been out vandalising the gents' urinal, couldn't she, Jack?'

'What? Yes, you could.'

'Dad, do I look the type to do an antisocial thing like that?'

'Looks don't come into it, Michelle. And don't try to make your father take sides. Up to bed with you this minute, and get the eight hours sleep a young growing girl like you needs.'

'But Mam, I've got business on first thing tomorrow.'

'Jack?'

'Better do as your mother says, Mike. I do – it's safer.'

So Mike, the queen of the wrong'uns at the King's Arms, reluctantly obeyed her mother and went upstairs to bed to sleep for the next eight hours. Her parents also retired to get the little sleep they could in what was left of the night.

The church clock struck four. Little Piddlington finally fell quiet. The empty streets became the hunting grounds for foxes, owls and mice. The quarter moon shone through light clouds. Behind the clouds, the stars slowly turned in the arc of the skies as time inexorably headed towards the fateful day.

The King's Arms
affectionately known as 'The Queen's Legs'

The Vicarage

Chapter 3: Into Action

3 : 1

The song birds sang their hearts out in the dawn chorus around Little Piddlington, early on Thursday 15th September 1983. They rejoiced that the sun beamed from a clear blue sky. All across the River Piddler valley, the natural world welcomed another late summer day.

As the clock struck seven, a harvest gold mini car drew up outside The Cottages to collect Mrs Smith and Mrs Blake. Driver Mrs Gwendoline Harty tooted as Jack Smith gave his wife an affectionate farewell. Jane Smith had glammed herself up even more than usual. In her hands she held a paper plate with slices from one of her prize-winning Madeira cakes. She drew back from Jack and trotted down the path, blowing air kisses.

'I must be going, dear. You will keep an eye on Michelle, won't you?' she said.

'Yes, dear. You have a lovely time in Bristol with the WI. Don't spend too much.'

She gave a last wave to him as she got into the back of the mini, joining Rosie Banner. Mrs Banner looked striking in her navy suit. She held a prize-winning chocolate gateau on a paper plate.

Mrs Jennifer Blake ran across from number 4, The Cottages, and climbed into the front passenger seat, ready to assist Mrs Harty with navigation should she get lost on the way. Mrs Blake looked a well-scrubbed version of her usual guider image. In her hands, she carried a prize-winning date and walnut cake on a plate.

Mrs Harty looked her usual no nonsense self in a grey twill suit. She tooted the car horn again to the audience of husbands who had come out of the cottages to wave their wives goodbye, and drove off down the road out of the village towards Effingham and Paddleham.

After the car had driven out of sight, the men turned to walk back up their front paths.

'We'll get a little peace now, eh,' said Gary Blake.

'Yes. At least it's a fine day for them,' Jack Smith replied.

Blake and Smith disappeared inside their cottages to finish their preparations for their different teams.

A short way across the green, Major Harty stood in the garden of thatched Rose Cottage. He turned to Ted Banner, who was standing in the garden of neighbouring Lilac Cottage.

'Good morning, Ted,' he greeted.

'Good day, Major,' Banner replied: 'A fine bright day for a community project.'

'I'll say. Dashed decent of the WI to give up having a go, what! How the ladies love their shopping!'

'Yes. It makes the odds so much better for us. See you later, Major.'

'I look forward to it, Chairman.'

3 : 2

Yes, the fateful morning had arrived in Little Piddlington. Already many of the villagers were busy finishing their preparations for the special day. Other people were making preparations too, further afield. In the Royal Mail depot at nearby Paddleham, the works bell rang. Twenty pairs of boots ran across the tarmac yard to line up in front of the foreman. He checked off the workers' names on a clipboard in his hand. His team of twenty blue-uniformed men slouched untidily, but he had a ramrod straight back and his uniform looked freshly washed and pressed. He glared at them. As usual on a Thursday, two men were missing, though not always the same two.

'Come on, lads! Sorting doesn't take that long,' he shouted.

The men muttered a form of an apology and straightened their double lines.

'Where's the rest of you, then? This is the Royal Mail, remember, not British Rail!' he yelled.

The newest recruit, young Cooper, piped up, his fair face going pink with embarrassment.

'It's Bates and Belling missing, sir. Someone's locked them in the toilets.'

His colleagues muttered to him to shut up, and the man standing behind him gave him a surreptitious kick in the ankles.

'Quiet, lads,' the foreman cautioned, well used to the men's Thursday morning behaviour. 'Now, before I give you your routes, I must take time to go over complaints again.'

He paused and turned over a sheet on his clipboard.

'Right, we received fifty-three complaints yesterday, all of them justified, and three of them up to National Certificate standard. Excellent work, all of you! Depot award for third place goes to regular Brian Bibby, for delivering all the Tory by-election addresses to the Friends of the Earth paper recycling unit. Second place goes to John Jackson and Ian Anderson for playing football with a box marked fragile and containing one Ming vase, uninsured. And first place deservedly goes to Danny Dalton, for successfully delivering the post to the RSPCA local office after biting off the ear of their Crufts champion Alsatian when it tried to bite him. Well done, lads, and keep up the good standards – we're in the running for the British Open Post Box Shield.'

The men clapped and cheered. Those nearest patted the backs of the four winners. The foreman let them celebrate briefly before raising his arms to quieten them down.

'Back to work, lads. Rotas. Any volunteer for Route 19?'

'I'll do it, sir,' offered young Cooper.

'Crawler,' muttered one of his colleagues.

'You can tell he's new to the job!' said another.

'That's to Little Piddlington, you berk!' another warned.

'Sorry, Young Cooper, you haven't completed your Delivery Drivers Combat Training yet. Anyone else for Route 19?'

Two more pairs of footsteps ran across the tarmac. The squad looked back as the much-delayed team of Bates and Belling turned up for the roll call.

'Sorry we're late, sir,' said Bates.

'Someone locked us in the toilets,' said Belling.

'A likely excuse! I hear that every week. Right, Route 19, Bates and Belling.'

'Oh no!' Bates cried. The colour drained from his face.

'Permission to go and make our wills first, sir?' requested Belling.

'Permission granted. Will forms are in the office. Jackson, Anderson, go with them, to witness they don't do a bunk.'

'Yes, sir!' replied Jackson and Anderson.

They marched the hapless Bates and Belling back across the courtyard to the office.

'Right, the rest of you: Route 1, Cotterell and Cooper; Route 2, Bibby; Route 3...'

3: 3

Meanwhile, Mrs Harty's harvest gold mini rattled down the road from Little Piddlington towards Effingham and Paddleham, en route to Much Muckleham RAF Base. The road wound through the fields in a series of sharp bends. As the car lurched from corner to corner, its three passengers struggled to keep hold of their prize-winning cakes. They had brought these along, intending to use them to bribe the RAF Base staff.

'Five miles from the village, and thirteen to go. We can talk now,' said Mrs Harty.

'Ooh, isn't this exciting?' said Mrs Blake.

'I said talk, Mrs Blake, not chatter like schoolgirls!'

Mrs Blake blushed. 'Sorry, Mrs Harty.'

A cream and olive green pantechnicon van passed the mini, heading in the opposite direction. From inside the van came the sounds of people warming up brass band instruments.

'Hey, isn't that the Down Effingham Brass Band van?' said Mrs Smith.

'That was, Mrs Smith,' Mrs Harty replied.

'And what would a brass band be doing heading for Little Piddlington?' Mrs Banner demanded.

'A good question, Mrs Banner; but we have more important

things to discuss right now. Time to distribute our tackle. Who wants to start?'

The ladies juggled with their cakes and the contents of their handbags.

'I will,' said Mrs Banner: 'One copy each of *Teach Yourself to Fly a Helicopter*: a bit out of date, so they don't cover Sea Kings, but they give you the gist.'

She handed out the yellow and black books individually with her left hand while her right hand kept the prize-winning chocolate gateau out of danger.

'Excellent. Mrs Smith?'

'Four spare bike chains from Mike's bike, in case of trouble.'

She put her prize-winning Madeira cake on the back parcel shelf so that she could hand round the bike chains. The evening before, she had taken time to clean the chains while waiting for her daughter Mike to come home from the King's Arms. Her husband Jack had not thought to question what she was up to: he assumed she was being exceptionally house proud.

'Good. Mrs Blake?'

'Four Girl Guide first aid kits for incapacitating the Sea King crew if necessary.'

She put her prize-winning date and walnut cake on her lap and handed out the small red pouches with their distinctive white crosses.

'Good. And I have brought along, four pairs of PC Tanner's handcuffs. But watch out, because I haven't got the keys,' said Mrs Harty. 'I see you have excelled yourselves in the cake baking department, ladies. If those prize-winning beauties don't tempt the Sea King crew men from their posts, I don't know what will!'

The mini passed a column of white-clad Morris Men dancing in procession to accordion music, led by the Fool who was dressed in a short green kirtle and a jester's cap. The team was heading along the road in the opposite direction.

'Hey, isn't that the Up Effingham Morris Team?' said Mrs Smith.

'That was, Mrs Smith,' said Mrs Harty.

'And what would a Morris team be doing dancing towards Little Piddlington?' demanded Mrs Banner.

'A good question, Mrs Banner; but we have more important thing to discuss right now.'

They continued to discuss their plan of action as the car passed through Effingham and Paddleham onto the Somerset Levels. Mrs Blake struggled to find enough of a break in the conversation to give adequate directions. In the end she had to shout to prevent Mrs Harty from overshooting the junction for the RAF Base.

'Right here! Now!'

The brakes squealed. Mrs Harty turned the corner so suddenly, the chocolate gateau flew out of Mrs Banner's hands and met a sticky end, squelching into the car window beside Mrs Smith.

'Sorry, ladies,' said Mrs Harty.

'That's the prize-winning chocolate gateau gone,' said Mrs Banner with a sigh.

Mrs Smith scraped a fingerful of gateau from the window and put it in her mouth.

'Mmm, it tastes lovely! Can I have the recipe, Mrs Banner?' she asked.

'Not now, Mrs Smith: that's the gate ahead,' said Mrs Harty. 'Action stations, ladies. Good luck.'

Mrs Smith took her prize-winning Madeira cake off the back

shelf and Mrs Blake lifted up her prize-winning date and walnut cake, ready for action.

The mini squealed to a halt. The Madeira cake flew out of Mrs Smith's hands and disintegrated against the back of the driver's seat.

'Sorry, ladies,' said Mrs Harty.

'That's the prize-winning Madeira gone,' said Mrs Smith.

'Quiet, ladies!'

A uniformed sentry came out of the guard box by the gate, looking smart in his blue uniform and peaked cap. He halted by the mini's front passenger door.

'Ooh, doesn't the sentry look handsome in his uniform?' said Mrs Blake, love-struck.

'Well, open the window for him!' ordered Mrs Harty.

Mrs Blake wound down the window with great energy. The sentry bowed down to speak to the car occupants, his face only inches from her. His nearness made her shake and perspire as if she were experiencing a menopausal hot flash.

'Good morning, ladies. Welcome to Much Muckleham RAF Base,' he said.

'Good morning, officer,' chorused Mrs Harty, Mrs Banner and Mrs Smith in reply. Mrs Blake looked as though she were about to pass out. Mrs Harty had to lean over her to respond.

'We're members of the Little Piddlington WI. Commander Millet-Airey invited us over.'

'Ah, yes: the Commander is expecting you. The green building on the right.'

'Thank you,' chorused Mrs Harty, Mrs Banner and Mrs Smith. Mrs Blake could only manage a giggle and a squeak.

The mini raced off, screeched round a corner and squealed to an abrupt halt. The date and walnut cake left Mrs Blake's clutches and flew out of her window. It landed with a squelch on the car park space beside her.

'Sorry, ladies,' said Mrs Harty.

'That's the prize-winning date and walnut cake gone,' said Mrs Blake.

'Now what will we tempt them with before we put the boot in?' asked Mrs Smith.

'I'm sure we'll find something,' replied Mrs Banner with a suggestive leer.

The four women scrambled out of the mini and stretched their bodies back into shape after their cramped journey.

They had parked next to a green single-storey building. The nearest door bore the sign 'RECEPTION'. Out of this door bounded Commander Millet-Airey, dashingly handsome in his blue RAF uniform, and with a lascivious look in his roving middle-aged eyes.

'Good morning, ladies. You're a fine, strapping bunch!' he greeted. An unwanted hand strayed where it should not go.

'Ooh! Commander!' objected Mrs Harty, raising her hand to slap his face.

Mrs Blake caught her arm to stop her and pulled her aside to place herself next to the Commander. His hand again strayed where it should not go.

'Ooh, Commander!' said Mrs Blake, giggling like a Girl Guide on a first date.

He gave her a sideways look and moved closer to Mrs Smith.

'Is this all of you, ladies?' he asked. An unwanted hand strayed where it should not go.

'Oh, Commander!' objected Mrs Smith, with a tired intonation that suggested she had to fend off such indignities so often it bored her.

'Sadly, yes, Commander,' said Mrs Banner. Her voice was low, warm and husky. When his hand again strayed where it should not go, she gave him a teasing smirk which turned her companions' heads in surprise. 'Ooh, Commander,' she hissed, 'You are a naughty boy!'

He beamed to find one of his visitors so clearly on his wavelength.

'I understand you would like a ride in one of our aircraft, ladies. What would you like a ride in first, eh? He, he, he!'

'Your kind invitation said a Sea King helicopter, Commander Millet-Airey,' said Mrs Harty.

'We've been so looking forward to it,' added Mrs Banner, her mouth open, her tongue caressing her upper lip.

'So have I, ladies,' the Commander said. 'If you would kindly step this way.'

'If I could step that way,' said Mrs Smith, 'I wouldn't need Jack's truss.'

'Ho, ho, ho! I like a bit of spirit in a woman!' said the Commander.

Mrs Smith firmly removed his straying hand from her derriere. He took out a hip flask.

'Here, have a snifter. It will help you relax,' he offered.

'No thank you, Commander Millet-Airey,' Mrs Harty firmly refused: 'We don't want to spoil our adventure by getting drunk, do we, ladies.'

'Oh, no, Commander,' chorused the others.

'It's only strong lemonade,' he said.

'Then later, perhaps,' Mrs Banner said, licking her lips.

The Commander escorted them between the single-storey buildings to the tarmac apron. Ahead of them, several large military aircraft had been parked up in clearly marked numbered spaces. Crews and engineers bustled around the aircraft.

'Are you married, Commander,' asked Mrs Banner in a low voice which sent an electric charge shooting down his spine.

'Only to the Air Force, Ma'am. But I do enjoy cheering up other men's wives, so do give me a ring if you feel like a little...' He broke off suggestively.

'Like a little what, Commander?' asked Mrs Harty, seeking clarification.

'Why, lonely, of course,' the Commander said.

'How about a little silly? I often feel like that,' said Mrs Blake. She feared Mrs Banner was leaving her far behind in the running for this uniformed hunk and thought a bit of girlishness might help improve her chances.

'Mrs Blake!' Mrs Harty scolded as though the Guider were still a teen.

The Commander stopped by an old bright yellow helicopter. Its rust-streaked matt paint made it look as if the Air Force had pensioned it off.

'Here we are, ladies. Our helicopter apron,' he announced.

'Is that a Sea King? It looks a lot older than I expected,' said Mrs Smith.

'Yes,' agreed Mrs Harty: 'Who would think an ancient thing like that could do so much in the Falklands last year.'

'That's not a Sea King,' said Mrs Blake: 'That's a Westland Whirlwind, a licenced British version of the US Sikorsky S55. Its livery shows it's been used for search and rescue.'

'Housewives, Mrs Blake,' hissed Mrs Harty in warning.

'Oh, so you know something about helicopters,' said the Commander. He looked at the Guider with renewed interest. His attention made her turn bashful.

'Not really. Just what I read in this book,' she replied, pulling out a yellow and black hardback book from her shoulder bag.

'*Teach Yourself to Fly a Helicopter*. He, he, he; I hope you're not planning to take one of mine,' joked the Commander.

'Oh, no!' 'We wouldn't dream of it.' 'Who us?' chorused the visitors.

'Only joking, ladies. That's the Sea King, over there. Let's climb aboard.'

He ushered them across to a larger, more modern helicopter in grey livery. The side doors stood open, giving access to the cockpit and the rear cabin. He helpfully gave each of the women assistance to climb inside. Mrs Blake was the first to enter.

'Ooh! Commander!' she gushed.

The visit continued. The members of Little Piddlington WI continued to endure and fend off the advances of over-friendly Commander Millet-Airey in the hopes of getting their free ride.

3 : 4

Back in Little Piddlington, the undertakers were preparing Mrs Holst for her last ride, one which she would fortunately know nothing about. As the church clock struck the half hour, the parlour room of number 2, The Cottages filled with musicians from the

Down Effingham Brass Band. The band wore a distinctive bottle green uniform with gold lanyards and epaulettes. The racket they generated as they warmed up their instruments was deafening.

'Half eight, Sam,' shouted Pete Green from the hall.

He had corralled the pallbearers and Jack Smith in the narrow hall passage. They all wore their best black funeral suits and ties.

'No need to remind me, Mr Green,' Sam McNab shouted back from the living room. 'Where's the bleedin' Vicar? 'E's always late for bleedin' funerals. Oi, you lot, get your cornets off that coffin – you'll open the secret compartment.'

'Sorry, Guv,' the cornet players shouted back.

'Hey, Drum Major, what's your spirit level like?' shouted the Band Master.

The Drum Major checked the spirit level on the side of his bass drum.

'Still half full,' he said.

'Right then, lads: time for a quick one before the Vicar arrives.'

The noise died down as the men refreshed their cups. As they moved about, a page of sheet music fell out of the parlour onto the hall floor.

'Hey, you've dropped your score,' said Pete Green.

Sam McNab picked up the page and nearly choked.

'*Alexander's Rag Time Band*? You're not playing that at my funeral.'

'Course not, Mr McNab: we'll be playing it after Mrs Holst's,' the Band Master replied.

One Eyed Jed came to the front door to ask for his mate, Matt Holst. When he saw how full the house was, he doubled back and walked round to the back alley. He entered the house by the back kitchen door. Matt was sitting at the kitchen table with his hands over his ears.

'Arr, Matt; what's it like living with the Down Effingham Brass Band, then?' he asked.

'Bloody awful, Jed,' Matt said. 'I don't even know why they're here. I didn't order them.'

'Then let's get out of here,'

'How, Jed? I've been trying for the last half hour.'

'We can go the same way I came.'

Jed dragged him out through the back yard into the rear alley. They turned left and left again and emerged on the road running through the village.

Across the green, they saw the Vicar and Miss Hanson hurrying towards Matt's house. They doubled back and tried to hide behind the corner of the end house, number 1. The Vicar was too preoccupied to notice their dodge, but Miss Hanson's quick eyes did.

'I can't hold a funeral service like this, Miss Hanson,' the Vicar was saying: 'I look as well-endowed as Farmer Duncan's prize bull!'

'Any higher and the collecting box would make you look pregnant, which would be even worse!' she replied.

She had dressed for the occasion in a fetching floral frock and straw hat, with matching cardigan and an outsized backpack. She marched past number 2 to the end of the terrace to challenge Matt and Jed.

'And where are you two likely lads going?'

'Who, us?' asked Matt sheepishly.

They re-emerged from around the corner of number 1.

'Yes, you, Mr Holst,' said the Vicar. He eyed Matt's casual T-shirt and jeans in horror. 'Aren't you coming to your wife's funeral?'

'Nay: it's enough to pay for it,' Matt replied.

One Eyed Jed tried to deflect the Vicar's attention by asking about the big bulge he had under his cassock and surplice.

'What've you got under your hassock, Vicar?' he asked.

'Woodworm, Jed,' the Vicar replied, answering him literally.

'Woodworm?' Jed repeated, astonished.

'He means cassock, Vicar,' Miss Hanson said.

'Oh, ha, ha, ha, this?' The Vicar laughed falsely. 'A collection box for the church roof fund.'

'It must be a mighty large collection box,' said Jed.

'It's a mighty large roof, and a mighty large hole. Come on, Miss Hanson.'

The Vicar and Miss Hanson gave up on the reprobates and forced their way in through the front door of number 2, The Cottages. Their arrival let Sam McNab heave a great sigh of relief.

One Eyed Jed and Matt Holst strolled off up the road past the pub towards the gated footpath from the green to Lodge Castle.

'Har,' said One Eyed Jed, 'Now I see what Miss Susy sees in 'im!'

'Do you think he's up to summat, Jed?' asked Matt.

'Oh, I know he's up to summat, Matt, but I think it be summat different to what you're thinking.'

Ahead of them in the hedgerow by the gate, a pale flesh-coloured object emerged inch by inch. As they walked nearer, the object proved to be a lady's lower leg.

Jed paused and strained to look at the object. Matt saw what had caught his attention and strained his eyes to identify it too.

'Hey, be that a leg in that hedge yonder?' Jed asked.

'It is, Jed. You must have your patch on the right eye for once.'

'No, my patch is on my left eye, not my right. Left right, right wrong. Right?'

'Whatever you say, Jed.'

They walked closer to the leg in the hedge. As they drew near, the foot at the end of the leg waved to them. The high-pitched voice of a young temptress called out alluringly.

'Cooee, boys!'

They stopped to stare at the vision in disbelief.

'By, see them toes wiggle,' said Jed. His good eye was as big as a saucer. 'That leg's attached to that voice, that is.'

'I don't like the sound of this,' said Matt.

'I don't mind it.'

'Cooee! Over here, big boys,' called the seductress.

Her naked arm emerged from the leaves of the hedge and beckoned.

'Look at that arm, Jed. All the way up to the shoulder!' Matt said.

'And beyond, I think. Let's go see,' Jed replied.

'What about the Post Office?'

'That can wait! Opportunities like this don't happen twice.'

They raced towards the bushes. When they dived through the gate to see who was on the other side, the temptress had vanished.

'Hey, where's she gone?' Matt asked.

'Over here, boys, in my secret love nest,' she called.

They looked around, not knowing what to look for. All they could see were some trees and shrubs, wide lawns, the shingle path and a green wooden potting shed. They huffed in disappointment.

'Love nest? Bain't no birds nest here,' said Jed.

'Only a potting shed,' said Matt.

'Come on, boys. I'm waiting.'

The penny dropped.

'The potting shed!' they both cried out.

They dived in through the door. Plant pots cracked across their heads. They crashed to the floor, unconscious.

Miss Susy dived out of the shed and locked the door behind her. She had dressed for the day in a short-sleeved moss-green shirt dress and had tied her blonde hair back with a plain black hair tie. For once, her face bore no make-up. Her pursed lips looked thin and determined.

'Sleep well with the plant pots, boys. I've got other fish to catch now.'

She walked away, rubbing her palms together at the prospect of her next targets.

3 : 5

Freddie Farley had been watching Miss Susy's antics from the Lodge Castle grounds. He raced through the shrubs bordering the wall to join her as she walked away from the potting shed.

'Wow, Miss Susy! One team down already.'

'But several still to go, Freddie.' Her tone was matter-of-fact. All trace of the seductive siren had gone.

As they strolled through the bushes chatting, she heard rustling in the undergrowth behind them. She stood still and put her right forefinger to her lips to warn Freddie not to speak. After listening for a few seconds, she dived into a rhododendron bush and pulled out the protesting little brat of a boy, Joey K.

'Got you! Listening in again, Joey?' she said fiercely, shaking him by the ear.

'Let go of me, Cousin Susan! You're hurting me!' he squealed.

'Good. Freddie, take his catapult!'

Freddie looked at her, aghast.

'Before he hits your vitals!' she urged.

'Not my eyes!' he said.

He snatched the catapult out of the boy's hands just before Joey fired it at him.

'Hey! Give that back! It's mine!' Joey protested.

'Shut up, Joey, and talk,' Susy said, not realising the contradiction in her order. 'Where are your brothers?'

'At home, asleep. They were up all night, drinking with Mike Smith.'

'The Kelly boys and Mike Smith?' Her tone was disbelieving.

'And her henchmen Smiley Winters and PC Tanner. They didn't get home till four this morning. Mrs Smith gated her. And I was looking forward to playing decoy, too!'

'So their plan's off?'

'Sure, Cous. They won't wake up in time.'

'Great. Two more teams down. What about the Parish Council?'

'What about them?'

Miss Susy grasped Joey's other ear, making him squeal again.

'Miss Susy, you're hurting him!' Freddie protested, feeling sorry for the boy.

'You stick to your work, Freddie, and I'll stick to mine,' Susy ordered. 'The Parish Council, Joey?'

'I dunno: I tell you, I dunno. They didn't talk about their plan this week,' Joey squealed.

She eased her grip a little, and he explained, 'It was on rice paper, and they ate it. I 'ate rice paper.'

'Come on, Joey,' she retorted, and pulled on his ear again. 'I saw you this morning, spying on Ted Banner's cottage.'

'Ow, ow! All right, I'll tell you.'

She grabbed his shoulder and released his ear. His expression turned from fear to cheek.

'You've got nails like claws, Susan. Is that why Farmer Duncan keeps saying he fell into a gorse bush?'

She pulled his ears again and dragged him towards the potting shed.

'No, ow, let me go!' he wailed. 'They were pushing Mr Blake into a Telegram Sam suit two sizes too small, and your dad was tinkering up his motorbike. Please let me go.'

'Sorry, Cousin Joey. Freddie, open the potting shed!'

Freddie unlocked the shed door. As Susy dragged Joey towards it, the boy struggled more desperately. When he heard the groans of Matt Holst and One Eyed Jed inside, his voice raised to a scream.

'Let me go! Let me go!'

He tried to wrestle against her in the shed doorway, but there could only be one outcome. Miss Susy hit her cousin on the head with a plant pot. He fell unconscious to the floor, joining the two old reprobates.

Susy stepped out of the shed, rubbing her kicked shins.

Freddie bolted the shed door shut again. As they walked away, they could hear a helicopter in the distance. The sound was so commonplace on fair weather days, they ignored it and headed back to the green.

'Atta Girl, Susy. Who's next?' asked Freddie.

Her eyes glinted keenly.

'Whoever turns up next on the green.'

3 : 6

The Sea King helicopter had left Much Muckleham RAF base and was heading towards Little Piddlington. The two RAF pilots sat at the Sea King's controls, while Commander Millet-Airey entertained the four WI ladies in the rear compartment.

'What a magnificent view, Commander,' vamped Mrs Banner, with seductive eyes.

He was momentarily transfixed.

'What? Oh, yes, the view. That's why we use helicopters, Mrs Banner. Mind, you're a fine view yourself!'

A hand strayed where it should not have gone.

'Ooh! Commander,' said Mrs Banner with reproving yet approving eyes.

'Do you think I could sit in one of the pilot seats?' asked Mrs Blake with great enthusiasm. 'I'd love someone to take a photo of me to show the Girl Guides where we've been.'

The Commander gave the instruction. The pilot on the right left the cockpit so that she could take his place. As she passed the Commander, a hand strayed where it should not have gone.

'Ooh, Commander,' she gushed, totally entranced.

'Look, Mrs Smith. There's Little Piddlington,' said Mrs Harty, pointing out of the window.

'So it is, Mrs Banner,' Mrs Smith replied. 'Oh, I can see our houses. And there are the Morris Men we passed.'

'They've almost got there,' said Mrs Harty.

Mrs Blake strapped herself in and smiled at the pilot on her left who was flying the helicopter. She asked him to tell her about all the controls. Despite his condescending tone, she paid careful attention to everything he said.

'Can you see the Post Office van yet, ladies?' asked Mrs Harty.

After a pause, Mrs Smith called out, 'Yes! It's just turned off the road from town.'

'Right on time! Out with the bike chains, ladies!'

Out from their handbags came the bike chains. Their move was so sudden, they caught the three men completely off guard. Three bike chains wrapped tight across the men's throats, choking their cries. Mrs Smith captured the pilot at the controls, Mrs Harty captured the pilot who had given up his cockpit seat for Mrs Blake, and, sweet revenge, Mrs Banner overcame the lecherous Commander.

Mrs Harty looked around for something to handcuff them all to, and spotted a convenient red-handled lever.

'Chain them to this handy handle,' she ordered.

'Not there!' cried the Commander, his voice barely audible with the bike chain wrapped around his throat: 'That's the short haul cargo belay release lever.'

Before he could finish croaking, the three women had

handcuffed the three men to the belays. Mrs Harty pulled the lever.

The three men catapulted out of the helicopter in the wake of a packing case roped on the same line. Their strangled cries grew distant as they fell. They landed with a splash in the oily waters of Spinney Pond and passed out among the fly-tipped washing machines and cars.

'Oh! Where have they gone?' asked Mrs Smith in indignant surprise, her First Aid kit at the ready. She looked out the Plexiglas side window as the hatch closed again.

'Ah, better than we had planned: we've dumped them all as cargo,' Mrs Harty said. 'Mrs Blake, take over the controls. Mrs Banner, assist.'

Mrs Banner joined Mrs Blake in the cockpit. Mrs Blake repeated what the pilot had told her about the controls, but it was clear the information was too technical for Mrs Banner to grasp.

'Mrs Smith, radar,' ordered Mrs Harty. 'I'll guide you in.'

'How do you do radar?' asked Mrs Smith.

'Just make sure we don't hit any of the white dots, Mrs Smith,' said Mrs Blake.

Her hands were rather full at that point. The Sea King was turning tight circles in the sky. The centrifugal force threw Mrs Smith and Mrs Harty against the rear compartment walls. It dawned on Mrs Blake that flying a helicopter was not as easy as the *Teach Yourself to Fly a Helicopter* book had suggested.

'Why are we going round and round?' gasped Mrs Harty.

'Give us time, Mrs Harty. You can't just step into a strange military helicopter and get it all right first go,' Mrs Banner said.

Mrs Blake persuaded the helicopter to stop spinning. Then

she spotted a large red button among the bank of switches to her left.

'I wonder what this is for,' she said. Curiosity got the better of her. She pushed it.

A warning buzz sounded. The helicopter fired a torpedo, making it jolt in the air. The torpedo hit the ground and exploded. Its aftershock made the helicopter buck again.

'You've just blown up Farmer Duncan's silage pit, Mrs Blake. Try to be a bit more careful,' chided Mrs Harty.

'Sorry, Mrs Harty. We're getting the hang of it now,' Mrs Blake replied.

She spoke too soon. The helicopter tilted to a rakish angle and then flipped. While Mrs Blake and Mrs Banner stayed put, safely strapped into the pilots' seats. Mrs Smith and Mrs Harty did not. The flip flung them onto the rear compartment roof. Mrs Smith swore as they picked themselves up and tried to stand. For once, Mrs Harty did not tell her off: the language she had been thinking was similar and worse.

'I never knew a helicopter could fly upside down,' said Mrs Blake.

The helicopter flipped again, throwing the two women in the rear compartment back down on the floor.

'Got her the right way up now too,' said Mrs Blake.

'I feel sick,' said Mrs Harty.

'Directions please,' asked Mrs Banner.

'Left a bit,' said Mrs Harty. 'Where's the brown paper bag?'

'In my handbag,' replied Mrs Blake.

Mrs Harty found the bag but had only opened it when she vomited. The remains of her breakfast splattered over the contents.

'I meant, the brown paper bags were in my handbag, Mrs Harty,' said Mrs Blake, having long had to accept similar behaviour from her Guides.

'Directions, please!' ordered Mrs Banner.

Mrs Smith leaned past the back of Mrs Banner's seat to look out of the cockpit window.

'Er, right a bit – we're over the pond. That's it: hover.'

Around the pond below them stood the small spinney. Four women came to the edge of the trees and waved.

'Look, there's the B team waiting for us,' said Mrs Smith.

'Yoo hoo! Hello-o,' called Mrs Blake, and waved with Mrs Smith. The helicopter lurched erratically.

'Stop waving, Mrs Smith, and tell us where to go next,' ordered Mrs Banner.

The women on the edge of the copse started shaking their fists. One clutched her near-naked head.

'Perhaps you should rephrase that, Mrs Banner. B Team's telling us where to go in no uncertain manner,' said Mrs Blake.

'Who do they think we are? Just because Mrs McNab's lost her wig in the downdraft,' Mrs Banner said. She shouted down at the B Team, 'It's not easy, flying a Sea King, you know.'

'Is that why you've got your eyes shut?' Mrs Blake asked her.

'No: I'm flying blind,' she quipped.

Mrs Harty had recovered a little but still felt very groggy.

'Please put us down, Mrs Banner, Mrs Blake. Farmer Jones' black field.'

'That's next to the pond, Mrs Smith,' Mrs Blake added,

trying to be helpful.

'I know, I know!' Mrs Smith replied. 'Forward twenty yards... Diagonally left four yards... another yard... and down.'

'We're landing,' squeaked Mrs Blake, almost overcome with excitement.

The helicopter touched down on the wet soil of the black field. It did not stop descending. Mud flew in all directions as it sank into the field.

'Oh, no! What's happening now?' asked Mrs Harty, alarmed.

'I don't know. We don't seem to be stopping,' Mrs Blake replied.

'There's mud all over the windows. I can't see a thing,' said Mrs Smith.

'Our rotor blades must be driving us down into the ground,' said Mrs Banner.

'You mean, into the bog. Do something!' Mrs Harty ordered in despair.

'I'm trying to,' said Mrs Blake. 'How do you switch this thing off?'

'If you don't know, Mrs Blake...' said Mrs Banner.

'Lift her up, lift her up,' cried Mrs Harty.

'I'm trying. She won't go,' Mrs Banner replied.

Mrs Smith spotted a red box with a glass cover set into the cockpit roof. She punched the glass with the heel of her hand, breaking it to reveal four glass tubes. Hoping the tubes were fuses, she pulled them all out.

The engines stopped. The rotor blades slowed down to a halt. After the noise of the flight, the silence was deafening.

'How did you do that, Mrs Banner?' asked Mrs Blake.

'I didn't,' Mrs Banner replied.

'I must have found the fuse box,' said Mrs Smith.

The blissful silence was soon disturbed by glugging sounds coming from outside. They realised their problems were not over. The Sea King was settling into the bog.

'I think our plan has gone wrong, ladies,' said Mrs Harty in defeat.

'What do you mean, gone wrong?' asked Mrs Blake, brightly. 'It's only a little mud over the cockpit windows. We just open the hatch, let in B Team, and fly off again.'

'Don't you realise what will happen when we open that hatch, Mrs Blake?' said Mrs Harty.

'No.'

Mrs Blake reached for the switch to open the hatch.

'Don't do it,' shouted Mrs Banner.

Too late. The hatch opened. Bog water and mud poured in.

'Oops! Now I do,' said Mrs Blake. 'Sorry, girls.'

The others gathered around her in the cockpit to shout.

'Help! Get us out of here! Please, help!'

Lilac Cottage and Rose Cottage

Chapter 4: Final Assault

4 : 1

Along the road to Little Piddlington danced the eight men of the Up Effingham Morris Team. They stepped in time to the reel played by their three musicians, the concertina squeezeman, the fiddler and the bodhran drummer. They were all dressed in white shirts and trousers. The dancers wore red caps pinned with plastic flowers, braces and bell pads. They had white handkerchiefs hanging from their pockets and long flower batons in their hands. The musicians wore embroidered waistcoats and tall black hats decorated with flowers. The Fool wore a green kirtle over his white trousers and a red and yellow jester's hat.

The jaunty music as they stepped through the travel dance over the last few yards into Little Piddlington, was momentarily drowned out by the noise of the Sea King helicopter falling from the sky into the field on the far side of the village.

'Did you see that helicopter come down, Morris?' asked The Fool.

'How could I miss it, Morris? It was very close,' replied Morris Bill.

'It was that! I'm going to write to that RAF base again. I've had enough of their noisy capers!'

When the helicopter fell silent, they could hear a nearby brass band warming up. Its B flat music clashed discordantly with the

Morris music played in the keys of C and G. The brass warm up evolved into a rough first rendition of the Death March.

'Is that a brass band I hear?' asked The Fool.

'I do believe it is. Doesn't that cornet remind you of something?'

'It certainly does! Our arch-rivals, the Down Effingham Brass Band. Come on, men: we're almost there.'

The pace of the travelling dance increased as the Morris team raced towards their goal.

A short distance away around the corner, outside number 2, The Cottages, their rivals the Down Effingham Brass Band went into formation for the Death March. The Drum Major took the beat from the Band Master and led the band off across the street towards Church Lane. Pete Green tried to call them back.

'Hold it, Band Master. The bearers haven't got the coffin out yet,' he shouted.

At first they did not hear him. Their pace sped up as they entered Church Lane. Pete called them back again, twice.

It took the third shout for the Band Master to hear him. He raised his mace to signal to the band to halt and turned on the spot to face them. The Drum Major stopped dead in front of him. Behind the drum, the cornet players skidded to a halt in surprise. The musicians behind them had not been watching the Master: they cannoned into the cornets and ended up in an untidy heap. The Death March staggered to a messy halt.

In the silence that followed, they heard the footsteps of the Morris men and the music of their reel as the Team turned the corner into the village.

'Is that Morris music I hear?' asked the Band Master.

'I do believe it is,' replied the Drum Major. 'Doesn't that squeeze box remind you of something?'

'It certainly does – our arch-rivals, the Up Effingham Morris Men. Come on, Band!'

The Drum Major struck up a sprightly marching beat. The brass players leapt to their feet. His mace aloft, the Band Master gave the signal to march forward.

'What about Mrs Holst?' called the Vicar from the doorway of number 2, The Cottages.

The brass band ignored him. They restarted the Death March at an extremely brisk tempo and marched off towards the church.

'Sorry, Vicar,' Pete Green apologised, red-faced. 'Pallbearers, follow that brass band!'

The bearers piled out of the house with Mrs Holst's coffin at a rakish angle on their shoulders. They raced off after Pete Green and the brass band. The Vicar chased after them, struggling to find the right page in his Book of Common Prayer.

'*We brought nothing into this world...*' he began, and promptly lost the page.

The Fool led the Morris musicians and the Team into the village. With a coffin crossing the road in front of them, he realised the brass band was marching to the church. He led the Team across the village green to head off the brass band. The two groups collided outside the lych gate and turned to face each other.

'Flower batons forward!' shouted The Fool.

'Trumpets, sound the charge!' ordered the Band Master. The trumpeters gleefully obliged.

'Up the Up-Es; down the Down-Es! Charge!' chanted the

Morris Men. They ran towards their rivals like rugby forwards.

They clashed on the green. The air filled with the rowdy noises of battle: men shouting, punches thudding, batons striking instruments, and instruments striking back. The battle spilled out over the lane between the church and the village store.

Above the clamour piped the shrill voice of the Vicar as he tried to keep up with the coffin.

'... *and it is certain we can carry nothing out. The Lord gave, and the Lord hath taken away. Blessed be the name of the Lord*!'

He dodged to one side to avoid a confrontation between the triangle player and the bodhran player.

'Take that, Morris!' shouted the triangle player.

He hit the bodhran player on the head with his triangle. It went 'ting!'

'Oyah!' cried the bodhran player.

He retaliated by giving three sharp whacks with his padded wooden tipper. The triangle player dropped like a stone.

The Vicar continued to dodge danger as he followed the coffin through the brawl.

'*I am the*... oops, *resurrection and the life, saith the Lord. He that believeth in me, though he were dead;* missed! – *yet shall he live*...'

The melee spilled out onto the road past The Cottages. A Royal Mail security van drove into the chaos, tooting its horn.

'The van, the Post Office van is here!' shouted Pete Green.

The news raced through the crowd of brawlers. Most turned from fighting to gather around the van. They tried to stop it by banging on its sides and standing in front of the bonnet.

Bates and Belling shouted back at them from the van as they

inched forward, punctuating their words with V-signs and other hand signals.

'Gerroff, you buggers! Let the Royal Mail through!'

Across the green, near the automatic urinal, a cornet player spotted the Vicar valiantly trying to lead the laden pallbearers to the church. He let fly with a fist. The Vicar dodged his surprise right hook.

'Bless you, my son: you'll have to be quicker than that. *And whosoever liveth and believeth in me shall never die.*'

Sam McNab appeared in front of the Vicar, having lain in wait for him in the urinal to take him out of the competition.

'Sorry, Vicar,' he said.

He punched him in the collection box and almost broke his knuckles.

'Ouch! A wooden jockstrap?' McNab said, swearing.

'*Et tu*, Sam McNab?' the Vicar replied.

The undertaker floored him with an uppercut to the chin. The Vicar dropped to the ground. Horrified, Miss Hanson punched McNab in the groin. He fell back onto the grass, poleaxed. The euphonium player put Miss Hanson out of action with a karate chop to the neck. Then he went to hide in the yard behind the pub.

On the other side of the green, the Royal Mail van managed to break free of the crowd. It accelerated towards the Gatehouse and the Lodge Castle drive.

'The van's got away!' shouted Morris Bill.

The Morris men ran off after the van. The brass band men chased after and waylaid them outside Lilac Cottage. While their attention was diverted, Miss Susy ran out from the Lodge Castle footpath gate with Freddie Farley at her heels. They crossed the green to the Vicar's side. He was lying senseless on the road by the pub.

Susy bent down and took hold of the Vicar's left arm to pull him up.

'Freddie! Grab his other arm.'

'You're not putting the Vicar in the potting shed!'

'Of course I am. He's one of the ringleaders.'

Freddie hoisted the Vicar's right armpit onto his left shoulder. Between them, they dragged the senseless priest along the lane and through the footpath gate. They tossed him in the potting shed with Jimmy K and the reprobates.

'That's another down, but we still need to be quick, Freddie: we've still got McNab and Miss Hanson to get.'

The melee had sprawled across the edge of the green between the road and the gate. Around the gate raged a free-for-all bare knuckle fight. Susy and Freddie had to dodge some stray punches to reach the senseless undertaker, McNab.

A Honda CB250 motorbike emerged from the back of Rose Cottage, forcing its way through the battle. Gary Blake struggled to control the bike with his arms constricted by a telegram uniform two sizes too small. He wove precariously through the brawlers and turned up the road to the Gatehouse.

The sheer physical effort of the battle began to tire the brawlers. More words were exchanged as fewer punches were thrown.

'You've trampled my trombone!' cried a band member.

'You broke my flower baton,' a Morris man replied.

'The Drum Major's walking very strangely,' said the flugelhorn player.

'Someone's put his drumsticks where the sun don't shine!' a trombonist replied.

The brawlers drew back, panting. Men dropped to the ground to rest. The two sides created a ragged circle on the grass. Soon, just two men were left standing in the centre of the circle. The Band Master faced up to the Morris Fool for a final showdown on the grass.

'At last, Band Master: we meet again!' said The Fool.

'You, Morris? Over my dead body,' the Band Master replied.

They circled inside the space created by their men, their bodies facing each other, their unblinking gaze fixed on each other's eyes.

The Band Master threw away his mace. The Fool reciprocated and threw away his flower baton. Like fighting cocks raising their feathers in challenge, the two men rounded their shoulders to make their muscles look big.

They plunged forward together to take each other in the same wrestling clinch. Their heads clashed: they fell to the ground, stunned. Their furious followers sprang back to their feet and surged forward once more. The battle recommenced.

One by one they fell. Miss Susy and Freddy picked up the fallen and dragged them off to incarcerate them in the shed. Soon, just a few of the largest men remained on the field. The brawling had so exhausted them, they gave up and lay gasping on the grass. As they were too heavy to be shifted, Susy and Freddy moved through them, hobbling them with ropes. Once all had been incapacitated, the couple ran off through the gate onto the footpath to Lodge Castle.

4 : 2

The Royal Mail security van sped along the shingle driveway through the Lodge Castle estate and skidded to a halt outside the pretentious stone porch of the Victorian mini-mansion. Phil Farley came out to meet the van. He was wearing chain mail and a Norman-style steel helmet. Bates and Belling got out. Belling opened the back of the armoured van while Bates stood on guard.

'Good morning, Mr Farley,' said Bates: 'At least we have managed to get the cash to you this week.'

'Despite the pitch battle going on in the village square,' added Belling.

'And I'm very grateful, boys,' Phil replied. 'Mrs Farley is waiting for you at the counter.'

He watched the two men unload the modest green money bag. They carried it into the building through the side door that led straight into the Post Office. It only took them a few moments to hand over the cash. Still alert for danger as they came back out, their heads turned towards the sound of a distant motorbike drawing nearer.

'See you next week,' Phil said.

'Not if we can help it,' Bates replied.

Bates and Belling jumped back into their Royal Mail van and drove off back down the shingle drive. Just before they reached the trees, a Honda CB250 motorbike cut across the front of their bonnet as the bike took its rider for a surprise power ride. The bike flew across the lawns and skidded to a halt on the shingle in front of Phil Farley.

Gary Blake alighted, red-faced in a tight telegram service uniform. The grey twill tunic strained across his body in rigid creases and the silver buttons threatened to pop undone.

'Telegram, sir,' he said, breathless with the chest constriction.

'Who for?' asked Phil.

'Mr Philip Farley of Lodge Castle, sir.'

'That's me. Why, if it isn't Mr Blake. What are you doing in a uniform like that, Mr Blake?'

'Trying to deliver a telegram, sir.'

'Managed to get a job at last, then, have you?'

An ancient Daimler drove up the shingle drive and skidded to a halt outside the door.

'Er, yes. Wasn't I lucky.'

'I don't know, Mr Blake. The Post Office stopped the telegram service over a year ago.'

Out of the Daimler stepped Ted Banner, Major Harty, Sharkie Sharp and Farmer Duncan. They slammed the car doors after them.

'It's a very late telegram, sir,' said Mr Blake.

'Really? Morning, Mr Banner.'

'Morning, Mr Farley,' said Banner: 'Just collecting my pension.'

'Major Harty,' Phil greeted with a nod.

'Morning, Mr Farley. Pension, what,' said the Major.

'Morning, Farmer Duncan. No shot gun this week?'

'No, Mr Farley,' Farmer Duncan said: 'These kind gentlemen have explained how I don't need a gun to collect my pension, only my pension book.'

'And Sharkie Sharp! Come for your pension too?'

'I'm not that old yet, guv'nor. I needed a first class stamp, so these kind gentlemen gave me a lift over.'

'From opposite the far end of the path?' asked Phil, pointing to the footpath that led directly to the village green sixty yards away. 'Or have you moved, Sharkie?'

'What about the telegram, Mr Farley?' asked Gary Blake.

Ted Banner, Major Harty, Sharkie Sharp and Farmer Duncan walked away through the side door into the Post Office.

'What about the telegram, Mr Blake?' asked Phil Farley.

'Aren't you going to open it? It says you've won the pools.'

'But I don't do the pools.'

Phil Farley broke off to stare in disbelief as his potting shed staggered onto the lawn and wove across the grass in zigzags. Distorted familiar voices cried out: 'Help!', 'Let me out!', 'Where are we?' and similar more colourful remarks.

'Is that my potting shed?' Phil asked.

The shed gained momentum and charged blindly to the far side of the lawns. It collided with a mature chestnut tree and collapsed. More colourful remarks decorated the cries of 'Argh!'

'That WAS your potting shed,' said Mr Blake. 'Look, you might have done the pools a year ago, when this telegram was sent.'

'I've never done the pools. I'm not a gambling man.'

'Then it must be from Ernie. Your premium bond's come up.'

'No, I don't have any premium bonds either. I don't believe in gambling of any sort. That's odd about the potting shed.'

'If you don't believe in gambling, why do you run the Post

Office?'

'That's not gambling, Mr Blake. It's my service to our stricken community.'

4 : 3

The four Councillors entered the Lodge Castle Post Office with a suspiciously nonchalant air. Behind the counter, Mrs Farley knew at once that something was up. She had dressed for the day in protective clothing which made her look as if she had come straight off an American football pitch, complete with padded shoulders and a helmet with a visor grill, both in white and blue.

Sharkie Sharp was the first to face her. He leaned an elbow against the counter and pulled out a letter, his stance deliberately obscuring her view of the door to the rest of the house. The Major pulled out some long-nose pliers and inserted them in the keyhole of the door. A few swift turns of the tool told him the Farleys had left the key in the lock on the other side as usual. That would make his job a lot easier.

Behind Mrs Farley, on the work shelf at the back, lay the green money bag brought by Bates and Belling. It was still full. As the Major had planned, the Councillors had arrived too early for her to put the money securely away in the cash drawer.

'Can you do me a first class stamp to London, Annie: one of them picture sort, with all them soldiers on,' Sharkie asked.

'I'm sorry, Simon: we sold out of them in July. I've got some lovely British Garden stamps, came in at the end of August,' she replied. Her warm tone made the other Councillors look at the two of them in surprise.

' "Simon"?' repeated Ted Banner, in disbelief.

Sharkie dropped his head to one side to hide his blushing cheeks and scratched his right ear. Concealed behind him, the Major flicked his wrist. His pliers turned the key and unlocked the door.

'Yeah, me and Annie go back a long way, don't we, love,' Sharkie said, and gave her a wink.

'We certainly do,' she said and relaxed: 'Bobbing apples at the church fete, carving our initials on the bench by the pub. What happened to that bench, by the way?'

'It was surplus to requirements when we got the urinal installed. I got a good price for it, from someone over Bristol way. Happy days, eh?'

A clatter by the public entrance door made them both look across. Farmer Duncan had somehow knocked over the display of Post Office and Royal Mail leaflets, and the Girobank stands. He lay in a heap with leaflets and stands piled over him. Ted Banner rushed across to help him to his feet. Then he picked up the stands which were blocking the entrance door.

While the others' backs were turned, Major Harty slipped through the door into the rest of the building unnoticed. His swift and silent turn of foot, learned long ago in action, was totally unexpected in a man of his age and appearance.

He stepped nimbly from black floor tile to black floor tile until he reached the door into the Post Office counter. There he listened, opened the door a crack, and listened again. The other Councillors were doing an excellent job keeping Mrs Farley distracted.

Ted Banner saw the movement of the door and put an armful of leaflets on the counter.

'Here, let me sort these out for you, Mrs Farley,' he insisted loudly.

'So sorry to cause you all this trouble,' Farmer Duncan repeated. His stubby, calloused fingers scrabbled on the floor as he tried to pick up more of the fallen leaflets.

The Major opened the door a little further and stretched his left arm along the work shelf. He could not quite touch the green money bag.

'No, I'll need to sort the racks out myself!' Mrs Farley said, exasperated.

She started to turn. To stop her catching the Major red-handed, Sharkie called out to her and pulled his wallet from his jacket pocket.

'Annie! I don't know if you ever saw this, but I've kept it with me ever since,' he said.

She turned back to him and looked with interest. He held up an old 1960s photo booth print of the two of them making faces at the camera. The worn photo was in monotone, black fading to sepia.

'My goodness! Simon, I never realised you were that serious,' she said, bending over the photo to get a better view of it through the visor of her helmet. They launched into a long conversation that meandered down memory lane.

Sharkie's device gave the Major enough time to slip in behind her, replace the money bag with a similar empty one, and slip back out of the counter side of the Post Office. The Major silently shut the door before hiding the full money bag in one of his large pockets. Then he slipped back through the door into the customer side of the Post Office, locking it again afterwards with the long-nosed pliers.

Sharkie brought the conversation to a close by reminding Mrs Farley about the first class stamp. He happily settled for one of Sissinghurst Garden, and left with a smile and a wink.

The other three Councillors followed him out. This puzzled Mrs Farley, as only Sharkie had actually made a Post Office transaction. She busied herself tidying up the leaflets and then turned to empty the green money into the till.

4 : 4

Ted Banner, Major Harty, Sharkie Sharp and Farmer Duncan strolled nonchalantly out of the Post Office and got back into the Daimler. Phil Farley paused from his odd conversation with Mr Blake about telegrams to look up at them.

'Goodbye, Mr Banner, Major Harty, Farmer Duncan, Mr Sharp. See you all next week,' he called after them.

Their car made a fast getaway down the shingle drive.

'My, they were in a hurry! As I was saying, Mr Blake…'

The Lodge Castle burglar alarm burst into life, deafening their ears. Mrs Farley ran screaming out of the front door.

'I'd better leave you to it,' said Mr Blake.

He kick-started his motorbike and raced off down the shingle drive.

'See you, Mr Farley,' cried his receding voice.

'What about my telegram?' Phil called out after him.

'Phil, Phil, we've been robbed,' Mrs Farley screamed.

'What, dear? No, you've just had to pay out some pensions to the Parish Council.'

She became hysterical. Snippets of information bobbed about in the stream of verbal diarrhoea: leaflets, Sharkie, missing money, and a long-dead affair. The torrent of words calmed her down from incandescent to just very angry.

When the truth finally did engage in Phil's brain, it shocked him out of his complacency. His face became red and his fists clenched.

'What?' he exclaimed and ran inside through the porch.

He hopped across the black floor tiles into the counter side of the Post Office. There on the worktop shelf lay the empty green money bag.

'Are you sure you haven't just put the money away and forgotten it?' he shouted back to his wife over the deafening peal of the burglar alarm.

She went back behind the Post Office counter and pulled open the empty cash drawer. Behind her visor, indignation distorted her face. All the drawer contained was fifty-three pence in change and a spare eraser.

'Can you turn off the alarm, dear?' he shouted: 'I can't hear myself think!'

She looked at him blankly. He repeated the request, using sign language to illustrate it. After pointing to the vibrating red bell above them on the wall, he covered his ears.

She nodded and said, 'Yes, I can,' but did not move.

After a brief wait, he shouted, 'Then why don't you flaming

well do it?'

She looked blankly at him and then realised what he was asking her to do. Shaking her head, she opened the control box behind her and reset the alarm. The bell stopped. The noise still echoed in his ears for over a minute afterwards.

Anne Farley took off her helmet and placed it on the counter.

'Sorry, dear: I can hardly hear a thing with that helmet on. When the alarm rings, I have to turn off my hearing aid.'

He took a deep breath.

'Right dear, can you tell me, step by step, what happened here just now?' he asked.

She nodded and sat down on the stool behind the counter.

'Those nice young men, Bates and Belling, had just left when those four Parish Councillors came in. I put the money bag on the back shelf, ready to put it away. Sharkie Sharp asked me for a first class stamp. We talked about the village bench. Farmer Duncan knocked over the displays. Ted Banner helped him pick them up again.' She took a deep breath. 'While they were sorting out the leaflets, Sharkie showed me some old photos.'

Something in her manner made Phil look at her face. Her expression turned defensive. She had never told Phil about her previous relationship with Sharkie, and now was not a good time to begin.

'Go on, Anne.'

'I sold Sharkie the first class stamp, and he left. The others followed him out.'

'And where was the Major in all this?'

Realisation slowly dawned. Her hands covered her mouth. Somehow, while Sharkie had been taking her down memory lane with the photo booth pictures, the Major had reached over and taken the money bag. Phil reached the same conclusion and scowled.

'I see. So it was a distraction theft. While Sharkie Sharp was getting your knickers in a twist, and Farmer Duncan was wrecking the place, aided and abetted by Banner, our other Parish Councillor, Gary Blake, was outside talking to me, leaving the way clear for the Major to grab the bag. Telegram indeed!'

His glare made her feel guilty. She spoke to divert his attention.

'We must phone the police, Phil.'

'We must. But not before you tell me everything about you and Sharkie Sharp.'

She saw his pointing finger and gulped. In response, she triggered the alarm bell once more.

4 : 5

Half an hour later, Phil Farley sat in the hall of Lodge Castle with the phone by his left ear. His wife was hiding in the Post Office, relieved that her husband had accepted her half-truth of an unrequited teenage crush. She longed to tidy up the mess left by Farmer Duncan and Ted Banner, but Phil had ordered her to leave it so that the police could examine the room for evidence.

'Come on, Constable. What's keeping you?' Phil complained as the phone continued to ring.

Eventually PC Tanner answered the call. His voice sounded very tired.

'Hello, hello, hello. Little Piddlington Police House.'

'At last, Tanner. This is Phil Farley of Lodge Castle Post Office. We've been robbed!'

'Robbed? Impossible! We were all asleep,' Tanner yawned.

'Wake up, you dozy bat! I said, we've been robbed. The Parish Council stole the money while Sharkie Sharp was chatting up my wife. I was outside at the time, being distracted by Mr Blake who was trying to deliver a telegram while my potting shed ran around the lawn crying "help"!'

Tanner drew a deep breath. His manner changed to the tone he used when speaking to someone with mental health issues.

'Potting shed, eh? And a telegram? And Mrs Farley? Fine, Mr Farley. I'll be right over as soon as I come on duty. That'll be twenty-two hundred hours – I'm on night shift this week.'

'But this is an emergency, man!'

'Of course. Have you been to see your doctor lately?'

'Stop this shilly-shallying and get over here at once! Or I'll report you to your superiors!'

Tanner's voice became stern.

'Really, Mr Farley? May I remind you that threatening an officer of the law is a serious offence.'

'I... I...' Phil spluttered.

'Fine. I'll see you at twenty-two hundred.'

Tanner ended the call. Phil threw his phone receiver into its cradle in disgust.

'Well, that's the second thing to go wrong today,' he complained: 'I wonder what the third will be.'

At that moment, the front door swung open. Freddy ran in with Miss Susy beside him, their faces beaming. The door slammed shut behind them with a bang which made Phil jump.

'Hi, Mum, hi Dad,' Freddie greeted.

'What now!' Phil shouted.

'Careful, Phil: your heart,' Mrs Farley warned, coming out into the hall to greet her excited son.

'Have we got great news for you!' Freddie announced. Susy nodded in agreement.

'That's nothing to the news I've got for you,' Phil replied.

'Miss Susy's ended the Thursday Ritual!' Freddie said.

Phil's head swivelled round to stare at his son's girlfriend.

'What, you masterminded the Parish Council?' he asked in disbelief.

'No,' Susy said, puzzled.

'Of course not, Dad,' Freddie replied. 'Susy engineered a battle between all the thieves on the village green. Then she caught all the ringleaders and put them in your potting shed. How amazing is that?'

'So you were the one behind it all!' Phil bellowed. He glared at Susy. 'Do you realise that while I was watching that potting shed staggering about my lawns, our Post Office was robbed?'

'Robbed?' Freddie repeated, shocked. 'But how? We stopped them all.'

'Not all of them, dear. The Parish Council walked straight in and stole the lot,' his mother replied, leaving a great deal unsaid.

'Oh, no; Mrs Farley!' Susy managed to look crestfallen.

'So the Thursday Ritual has certainly ended, Susan; and your interference has certainly helped,' Mrs Farley said, her face grim. 'I've said often enough, if we were robbed again, the Post Office would close. So closed it just has, for good!'

'But Dad, what about this service to the community you keep telling us about?'

'Stuff the community! From now on, I'm looking after Number One. And myself,' Phil said. 'The Post Office goes, and the village will just have to suffer the consequences.'

'Yippee, Freddie. Then we can get married at last!'

Susy wrapped her arms around Freddie and gave him a long, passionate kiss.

'Married?!' exclaimed his parents in horror.

Freddie extricated himself from Susy's arms.

'Yes, married,' he admitted sheepishly.

'Freddie promised. If I helped end the Thursday Ritual. Which I have.'

'Perhaps I was a little hasty about closing the Post Office,' Mrs Farley said.

'And I was too,' Phil agreed.

The front door slammed open. Sharkie Sharp entered, cocking a twelve-bore shotgun.

'Going back on your word again, Farley? Like you did with Miss Hanson?' Sharkie said.

He pointed the shotgun at the painting of Monty Farley Nine and then at the most expensive-looking canvass on the walls of the panelled hall.

'Miss Hanson?' asked Mrs Farley, shocked.

Her blood began to boil. How could Phil have just accused her of betrayal because of an innocent teenage romance, when his own actions as a young man had been so much worse? She clenched her fists and took a menacing step towards him.

'You hypocrite!' she hissed.

Phil saw her demeanour and went pale. He quickly turned back to face Sharkie.

'Of course I wouldn't, Mr Sharp,' he fawned: 'A family as old as mine wouldn't dream of doing a thing like that, these days. Especially with a twelve-bore pointing at my reproduction Turner.'

Sharkie nodded with a knowing smile. He uncocked the shotgun, broke it open and hung it over his left arm.

'Knew you'd see sense, Phil. I'll go and see the Vicar about the banns. As soon as he gets back from hospital.'

And so, for Miss Susy at least, crime really was going to pay, at least when committed by others.

Lodge Castle

MAGGIE SHAW

The Morris Men at a Local Gala

Chapter 5: The Aftermath

5 : 1

The Parish Council held an emergency meeting at the King's Arms when the pub opened at lunchtime after the robbery. They used a side door to avoid the regulars in the Saloon Bar, who were discussing the heist, each wishing their team had carried out the successful raid. The Councillors gathered in the Snug Bar to divide their spoils.

'What a plan that was!' said Ted Banner. 'And perfectly executed.'

'I'd never have guessed you were so nifty with a lock, Major,' said Sharkie Sharp, deeply impressed by his skills. 'Maybe I should've joined up too.'

'You were pretty nifty yourself, what, distracting Mrs Farley with those photos,' the Major replied.

'Farmer Duncan and Ted Banner helped when they wrecked the display stands, giving me time to think,' Sharkie said.

'And don't forget, the top-ho performance from Mr Blake, keeping Mr Farley distracted outside,' the Major said.

When they had finished patting each other on the back, they started discussing how they should distribute the loot. It did not take long for them to discover their problems had only just begun.

Because they had previously minuted that no-one in the village should be left penniless after the theft, they first had to agree a list of all the beneficiaries, a minefield in itself. They spent the second hour trying to allocate payments from the loot sufficient for each beneficiary without penalising others. When this had not yet been resolved by the third hour, the patience of some of the Councillors was wearing thin.

'Look, this is getting us nowhere,' said Sharkie Sharp. 'I still say we should keep it all for ourselves.'

'I agree, Mr Sharp. How else will we fund our doggie lav?' said Mr Blake.

'Gentlemen, please!' ordered Ted Banner. 'We have already voted on the issue. It is minuted that we will not deprive the poor of the village of their food and drink, simply because Major Harty's excellent planning allowed us to beat the system.'

'Hear, hear,' agreed Major Harty.

'What about Mrs Kelly?' asked Farmer Duncan: 'You've only allowed 'er thirty pounds, and she's got them no good layabouts the Kelly boys to feed as well as 'er little brat Joey K.'

'Up it to fifty pounds, then,' said Ted Banner. 'Mind, give it to her, not them – they'll only spend it on snooker and drink.'

'That leave £180s in the kitty, Chairman,' said Sharkie.

'And Matt Holst, One Eyed Jed's missus, the Smiths, the Greens, Smiley Winters and myself still to pay,' said Mr Blake.

'Thirty quid for each family,' Ted Banner instructed.

'Thirty quid? That's less than my SS,' protested Mr Blake.

'Take it or leave it, Mr Blake. You do still have your Social Security cheque,' said Banner.

'And no place to cash it!'

He considered the options briefly and reluctantly agreed, 'Okay, I'll take it.'

Sharkie Sharp thumped three ten-pound notes on the table.

'Ten, twenty, thirty pounds to Mr Blake. Sign here, please.'

Mr Blake signed the receipt and pocketed the money.

'How much does that leave us with now, Mr Sharp?' asked Ted Banner.

'When we've paid out this lot, Chairman? Nothing. Precisely nothing.'

'But there must be something,' said Farmer Duncan; 'What did we do it for, if we got nothing?'

'Not even a Post Office,' complained Mr Blake. 'Not even my SS.'

Major Harty spoke up. 'We did it, for the spirit of the exercise. It's not the winning, but the taking part that counts.'

'That's not worth going to jail for,' said Sharkie: 'We can't even bribe PC Tanner.'

Farmer Duncan said, 'I propose we pay PC Tanner fifty pounds hush money out of Council funds.'

'Seconded,' said Major Harty.

'Motion carried. Clerk, write the cheque,' Ted Banner ordered himself. He took out the cheque book ready to write one.

'No, Clerk, cash the cheque,' Sharkie warned. 'You see, we wouldn't have to bother with Council funds if we'd kept it all in the first place. Help the poor, yes; but this village is stuffed to the rafters with poor: scrounging from door to door, putting things on the slate, ducking out of paying bills, tapping the better off...'

'Not all at once, I hope,' said Major Harty.

'It is a grave problem,' Ted Banner said. 'But, as you will all remember, we did ask the Community Action Sub-Committee to look into that issue. Major Harty, what were your findings?'

'I've been waiting for you to ask that, what,' said the Major: 'I've got another plan.'

'I hope it's not as good as the last one,' muttered Sharkie.

'It's even better,' Major Harty replied. 'Your rice paper envelopes, men.'

He handed out the envelopes. The Councillors opened them and read the contents. Murmurs of approval were heard.

Ted Banner voiced the official assent. 'What a plan, Major. Another winner. We look forward to putting this into action with you. All those in favour?'

All right hands were raised, and some left hands too.

'Passed unanimously. Now, let's get down to work.'

5 : 2

The day of reckoning for many of the people who had taken part in the last Thursday Ritual, was the day after the battle of Piddlington Green.

First to rise was Rev Paul Oldham. His guilty conscience had punished him with a sleepless night because of the part he had intended to play in the Ritual, despite his failure to commit the crime. He had got back from the first aid room in the Effingham Cottage Hospital, to find Sam McNab's pallbearers had abandoned Mrs Holst's coffin in a hastily dug open grave in the church graveyard. As the Vicar completed the interment the following morning with just Miss Hanson beside him to witness the rite, Sharkie Sharp strolled across the graveyard to join them.

The shopkeeper looked his usual shifty self. He eyed the

remorseful priest up and down as he waited for the ceremony to finish. When the Vicar finally turned away, he joined him.

'A word if I may, Vic,' he said.

'It's Paul, actually,' the Vicar said. 'Let's adjourn to the church.'

He handed his Book of Common Prayer to Miss Hanson and escorted Sharkie to the church porch, rubbing the soil from his fingers with a crumpled white handkerchief. He opened the door into the church with a massive blacksmith-wrought iron key. The heavy oak door creaked open, and a musty smell wafted out. The two men walked in and sat on neighbouring pews close by the entrance, near the back of the plain, whitewashed church.

'You look like the morning after the night before, Vic,' Sharkie said. 'Sorry our Susan packed such a punch. I'll get her to make it up to you.'

'No need, Mr Sharp. Thanks to Miss Susy, I ended up doing no wrong, despite myself. I don't know what came over me. I could have lost my parish.'

'Well, we all make mistakes. As nothing's come of it, you're in the clear. So forget it. You can help me instead.'

The Vicar looked up at Sharkie in surprise.

'Nah, nah, it's nothing like that,' Sharkie said, smiling. 'Freddie and our Susan want to get married. The Farleys finally gave their blessing yesterday lunchtime. When's the earliest you can read the banns?'

The colour drained from the Vicar's face. He felt abandoned. How could he live the rest of his life without Miss Susy's ministrations? Sharkie saw his change of expression and looked at him in concern. He hastily replied with the first appropriate answer that came to him.

'I'll have a look in my diary and get back to you, Mr Sharp.'

Sharkie patted the Vicar's hand to reassure him.

'No sweat, Vic: in your own good time. Looks like you need a few days off. I've got some great tonic I can send up to the Vicarage for you; no charge. No-one's ever said the Sharps don't repay their debts.'

Sharkie walked back outside into the September sunshine. Rev Paul Oldham continued to sit in the pew, reflecting on the indirect way God had found to punish him for his sins.

5 : 3

Further afield, others were also counting the cost of their day's jaunt in Little Piddlington. The musicians in the Down Effingham Brass Band had a huge repair bill for damage to their uniforms and musical instruments. The smaller Up Effingham Morris Team had a smaller but equally daunting repair bill for theirs. As the wedding and village show seasons were nearly over, neither band knew how they would raise the money needed.

The Royal Mail had come out of the ritual with little more damage than an odd dent to their van. The National Post Office took the loss from the theft, when the police did not take the crime seriously enough to investigate properly.

Phil Farley complained to his superiors about PC Tanner's reaction to his original complaint. The National Post Office reported the crime again, to Tanner's superiors at Paddleham Police Station. They thought that would make a difference. It did not. The Paddleham police issued a crime number so that the Post Office could claim on their insurance. Then they sent PC Tanner to take statements from the Farleys and the Parish Council. This was after the Parish Council had given him a bribe.

A few days later, Tanner sent all the witness statements he had collected back to Paddleham. By tea time that day, the station notice board had gained a cartoon of Phil Farley in full armour on a Honda motorbike tilting at a collapsing shed. A copy of the cartoon found its way into the case file. The case was closed the following day for lack of evidence.

The hardest hit was Commander Millet-Airey. The top brass above him had long known about his peccadillos. They had turned a blind eye to his antics before, believing them to be just the adventures of a regular Jack the Lad. Now that his weakness had led to the theft of one of their aircraft by four late-middle-aged women from the WI, they could do that no more. They dared not risk making the Royal Air Force an object of ridicule by prosecuting the four hijackers, because a court case would bring his lechery to the attention of the public and make heroes of the thieves. Instead, they gave the Commander an immediate sideways transfer to the Ministry of Defence. For the rest of his career, Wing Commander Millet-Airey was restricted to flying an office desk in Records.

5 : 4

Although the Post Office closed as an immediate consequence of the last Thursday Ritual, the remote village of

Little Piddlington was not left destitute for long. While one quaint country custom fell into disuse, another emerged to take its place.

The resourcefulness of men whose backs were against the wall and whose wallets were suffering, inspired new solutions to the problems of rural decay. Guided by Major Harty's impeccable strategic planning, the Parish Council created the Community Regeneration Scheme. The Parish Council applied to the Council for Small Industries in Rural Areas and opened a branch of CoSIRA in the Saloon Bar of the King's Arms. Ted Banner opened a business consultancy in the Snug Bar of the King's Arms. And Sharkie Sharp opened a satellite branch of the Somerset Central Bank in the Lounge Bar of the King's Arms. New businesses sprang up like mushrooms. Soon all the villagers were off the dole and living instead on grant money. The village entered a period of newfound affluence.

Phil Farley was well placed to take advantage of this. He opened a betting shop in the former Post Office and quickly won back his family's fortune. He made a financial agreement with the Vicar whereby he instructed the priest when to wear his collection box under his cassock, in return for a regular donation towards the church roof fund. Church attendance improved, as the gamblers turned up each service to see for themselves whether the Vicar was wearing the collection box that day. Other villagers also attended more regularly to speculate whether it really was a collection box at all.

Eight months after the last Thursday Ritual, on the morning of Friday April 14th just before opening time, Tom Oddfellow was behind his bar, practising for the lunchtime crowd. Smiley Winters stood near him at the end of the bar with a dustpan and brush.

'Same again. Coming right up.'

Tom chinked a bottle on an empty glass as if to fill it with whiskey. The glass slithered along the counter and fell off the end, smashing onto the floor. Smiley swept up the fragments and put them in a large plastic bag.

The pub door opened. Mike Smith strutted in, six feet tall in her platform boots, and looking good in her black leathers. She crossed the bar to speak to a man in a charcoal grey suit with a CoSIRA name badge that read Con Aldeigh. He was short and balding, and looked like a fish out of water. He sat at a table covered in documents and brochures.

'Morning, Mister. Are you the Government Grant Man?' she demanded.

'I am. And you are?'

She smiled and offered him her leather-gloved hand.

'Mike Smith, proprietor of the Little Piddlington Bits and Bobs Factory. My business needs a grant.'

'I see. What does your factory make?'

'This.'

Mike placed a block of wood in front of him on the table. She had picked up the water-stained object in Pond Spinney the day before. It looked valueless.

'That? But it's just a piece of wood, straight out of a junkyard,' he said.

'To you and me, maybe. But to the tourists? One natural country paperweight.'

She then placed a bag of broken glass on the table.

'I also make this.'

'But that's just a bag of broken glass.'

'To you and me, maybe; but to the tourists? One traditional country burglar alarm. Keep sweeping it up, Smiley.'

'Right, Mike,' Smiley said with a big grin. He poured more broken glass fragments into a plastic bag. All his Christmases had come at once, landing this job with the fiery young woman he had lionised since childhood.

'Same again,' said Tom Oddfellow; 'Coming right up.'

Chink, slither, smash went the glass. Swish, swish; pour went the fragments.

Con Aldeigh nodded as understanding dawned.

'Ah, so you and your employees make traditional rural craft items, Miss Smith. Then I'm sure we can find a grant for you.'

He scribbled some information on a pre-printed form and handed it to her.

'Take this form to Mr Banner's business consultancy in the Snug Bar. And don't forget to open a bank account – see Mr Smith in the Lounge Bar, third door on the left.'

'Thanks, pal.'

Mike walked off to the Snug Bar, clutching the forms.

'Another business making rubbish for the tourists,' muttered Con Aldeigh, shaking his head. 'Who cares? As long as I'm getting my cut.'

5 : 5

The pub offices closed early that day, as a cascade of bells pealed out from the church to summon the guests to the wedding of the decade.

At 3 pm precisely, Sharkie Sharp escorted his beautiful daughter down the aisle to where Freddie awaited her. The groom looked dashing in his grey morning suit with a daffodil buttonhole, and with his barber-tamed hair and beard. Susie looked stunning in her ivory velvet bridal gown, with her blonde hair and shoulders draped in a delicate veil of silk lace. Her page boy, little Joey K, had been relieved of his catapult that day, and looked dubiously angelic in his smart outfit of pale green knickerbockers with ivory stockings and shirt. The outfit made him want to vomit. He had already prepared his revenge.

The church was full to its newly repaired rafters. Susy had invited everyone who had taken part in the last Thursday Ritual in any form. The members of the WI and the Parish Council sat behind the Sharps on the bride's side of the church. The pub regulars, the reprobates, the gamblers and the undertakers sat behind Mr and Mrs Farley on the groom's side of the church. Missing were formal representatives from the local Air Force Base and the Paddleham Police Station, but PC Tanner attended with Bates and Belling from the Royal Mail beside him, all dressed in civvies. The Down Effingham Brass Band had been booked to play the hymns and processional music. Its members filled the choir stalls. The Up Effingham Morris Team had been booked to lead off the dancing after the reception in the vast decorated marquee on the Lodge Castle estate lawns. They sat at the back of the church, ready to leave the ceremony first to create a wedding arch with their flower batons for the bride and groom to process through after the ceremony. The fees for the appearances of both groups were enough to pay off all the loans they had taken out to get their uniforms and instruments repaired.

Rev Paul Oldham took the service. His voice was clear and encouraging. No-one saw the sorrow and regret he hid within as he pronounced Freddie and Susy man and wife.

The radiant couple walked together down the aisle to the stirring march chosen by the Band Master especially for the occasion: the brass band's newly scored version of Queen's recent hit: *Another One Bites the Dust*.

The Morris Team heard this as they raised their flower batons outside and immediately took umbrage on behalf of the bride and groom. They had been looking for the opportunity of a rematch with the Down Effingham Brass Band since the previous September. They held their baton arch intact as the congregation emerged from the church to the sounds of *The Dambusters* march. When the brass band followed everyone out playing Sousa's march, *The Liberty Bell*, the flower batons descended upon their bonneted heads and shoulders with venomous force.

The Vicar hastily intervened, trying to halt what he sensed was about to erupt. He sent the brass band to play more of their repertoire on the green while the wedding photographs were taken. Then he asked the Morris Men to make their way to the marquee, which they ignored. As The Fool argued with the Vicar, little Joey K hid among the gravestones, looking for the cache he had hidden there the day before.

The brass band processed to the green playing the theme from the film *Bridge on the River Kwai*. They were regrouping on the grass with the opening bars of *Drum Majorette,* the Match of the Day theme tune, when the Morris Men struck.

The village green became a battleground once more, as brass

band player fought Morris dancer, trying to settle old scores. Several villagers threw their jackets onto gravestones and ran down to pitch in.

Susy serenely watched the melee from the church porch as she posed with Freddie for yet more photographs. He smiled at her, happy that she had made this decision for him, with the help of her father's shotgun to persuade his parents. Now he would forever be able to paint in peace. Susy smiled back at him. She had got the security and status she had always wanted. Nothing would be allowed to spoil that.

Little Joey K raised his catapult from behind a gravestone and took aim at his cousin's £500 ivory velvet wedding dress. The elastic twanged. A homemade ink bomb shot off through the air towards Susy's shapely bodice.

THE END

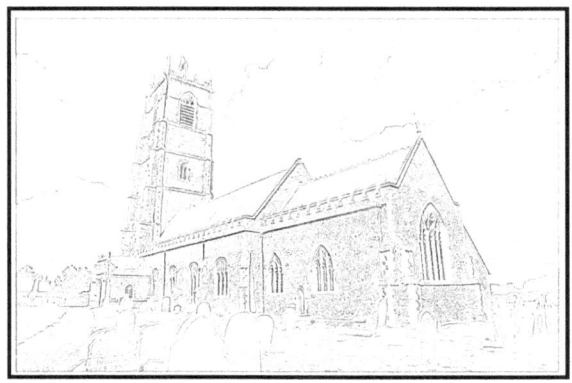

Little Piddlington Church

Thank You

Thank you for purchasing this book.

If you have enjoyed the story, it would mean a lot to us if you could rate or review it on the site where you purchased it.

Do visit our website www.eregendal.com to find out more about Maggie Shaw and our products. You can also sign up to our newsletter there and keep up to date about all that is happening in the world of Eregendal.

About the Author

Author Maggie Shaw creates her stories from her many and varied life experiences. A teenage runaway who made good despite undiagnosed Autistic Spectrum Disorder, Maggie writes as one who has walked the walk in recovery and spiritual development. Her degrees in science, divinity and church music, and her career as a Mental Health Dietitian, give a solid framework to the exciting adventure stories she loves to tell. The Scottish hills and Lakeland fells where her grandparents farmed often feature as landscapes in her work.

She is also a church musician, composer and song writer, and many of her songs are inspired by the stories she writes.

This is the fifth book Maggie has published through micropublisher Eregendal. Her other titles are *The Vision and Beyond* (2018), *Diviner's Nemesis I: Avenger* (2019), *Diviner's Nemesis II – Retribution* (2020) and *The Eagle and The Butterfly* (2020). She has broadcast music and short stories on Radio Carlisle, Cat Radio, and Red Shift Radio; and contributed articles to The St Raphael's Guild *Chrism,* The Chronicle, The Church of England Newspaper, and *Soul and Spirit* Magazine. Online, Maggie publishes through ArtSwarm, YouTube, Sound Cloud, Facebook and the Eregendal website www.eregendal.com.

Maggie lives in Cheshire with her husband Alan.

www.ingramcontent.com/pod-product-compliance
Lightning Source LLC
Chambersburg PA
CBHW070557180626
46817CB00005B/1878

* 9 781838 131333 *